'Are you plan
Eddie's death

'Don't be so melo
formidable.

Ace's brows rose in simulated surprise. 'What other reason could there be for a girl who looks like you doing your job?'

Kate felt fury well up in her. 'What an arrogant, narrow-thinking man you are!'

'I just wish I could be sure that your chosen career had nothing to do with the fact that it was mine!'

Dear Reader

As spring moves into summer, you can't help but think about summer holidays, and to put you in the right frame of mind this month's selection is jam-packed with exotic holiday destinations. As a tempter, why not try Patricia Wilson's new Euromance, DARK SUN-LIGHT, set in sultry Spain? *And*, who knows, you may well find yourself one day visiting the very places mentioned in the novel! One thing's for sure, you're bound to have lots of fun on the way. . .

The Editor

A born romantic, **Kristy McCallum** is lively, fun-loving and happily married to a very good-looking man. She has three children, three cats, one dog and other animals she adores. She lives in a particularly beautiful part of the West Country but it rains quite often, so travel to the sun features prominently in her plans. She hopes her readers share her belief that that special man should be kind, amusing and sexy, and passionately in love with her.

Recent titles by the same author:

SOMETHING WORTH FIGHTING FOR

DRIVEN BY LOVE

BY

KRISTY McCALLUM

MILLS & BOON LIMITED
ETON HOUSE   18–24 PARADISE ROAD
RICHMOND   SURREY   TW9 1SR

First published in Great Britain 1993
by Mills & Boon Limited

© Kristy McCallum 1993

Australian copyright 1993
Philippine copyright 1993
This edition 1993

ISBN 0 263 78038 4

Set in 10½ on 12 pt Linotron Times
01-9306-50446

Typeset in Great Britain by Centracet, Cambridge
Made and printed in Great Britain

CHAPTER ONE

'KATE? Carlisle Flint are having problems on the test circuit. They need the "liquid assistance of a fuel technician" like yesterday!'

The tall girl turned away from the screen she was monitoring to smile at her immediate boss. Jason was in charge of the team that was responsible for devising the new fuels always in demand by the competitors in Formula One Grand Prix racing. She had been working with IMP for just under a year now and had managed to contribute significantly to their joint effort, so she didn't feel quite as inadequate as she had when she first joined them.

For a start she had been the only woman, and her colleagues had found it strange that she should be working with them. Motor racing, or at least the back-up crews behind the competing teams, was traditionally male-dominated, and Kate was an eye-catching exception.

Five feet eight with natural platinum hair that fell straight on to her shoulders, she had a naturally curvaceous figure without really being overweight. What made her face so memorable, though, were the high cheekbones and the slanted dark brown eyes that were in such shocking contrast to her hair. Her looks were sufficiently unusual to attract a second glance in spite of an aloof and rather intimidating expression which she cultivated as a form of defence against being the recipient of too much male attention.

She thought it was from her father that she'd inherited her logical mind and a way with figures. She'd taken her degree in chemistry at university, and once she'd gained her doctorate had started work in one of the smaller fuel companies. Her choice of career had surprised and confused the students competing against her for jobs, but she'd never allowed the unspoken disapproval that had surrounded her to deter her from her goal. Maybe she had achieved her present position because she was a woman breaking into a man's world, but she wouldn't have survived or been so successful if she hadn't been good at her job.

She'd progressed from a rather lowly start to her present place on the team with IMP just at the time when the true importance of the fuel companies and their technicians was beginning to be appreciated by the general public, or at least those *aficionados* who followed the world of Grand Prix racing.

'So?' she queried, smiling. 'Does that mean you're off immediately?'

'No, not this time. I want you to go.' He gave her his normal rather contained smile. 'Come on, Kate. You've been with us nearly a year now, and it's thanks to your work that we're well on the way to managing the volatility problem at high temperatures.' His voice sounded rather grudging as he admitted her contribution. 'As you know they're testing in France at Paul Ricard because of the exceptionally hot weather there at the moment. . .'

Kate tried to control her unruly emotions as Jason continued to talk technicalities to her. She didn't want this, did she? She was part of a team and content to be just that; she didn't want to have to leave the protective colouring her job gave her in the safety of the laboratory.

'Just me?' she queried when he'd finished talking, her face giving little away of the tangled emotions behind its passive façade. She was surprised that he'd picked her in spite of her work. For some time now she'd had the feeling that she was not the flavour of the month as far as he was concerned.

'Just you,' he agreed, 'and you know why. We've got too much going on here at the moment.'

She bit her lip. 'Yes, I do know, but it'll be a pity if I have to abandon this present test I'm working on, won't it?'

'You won't. I'll look after it for you until you're back.' He answered a little too keenly, and Kate gave a small sigh. She knew he'd take the credit for her ideas; then she gave a mental shrug. Did it really matter? She was part of a team and pleased to have it that way. Jason, as if aware of her reservations, continued aggressively. 'Anyway, why be so averse to the trip? You'll only be there a couple of days at the most. The south of France is pretty high on people's agendas at this time of year. You've managed to dodge meeting the boys at the sharp end of this exercise for far too long. If they're whingeing because they haven't got quite the times they hoped

for, then let them complain into your shell-like ear
for a change. It might at least improve their
language!'

'OK, Jason. When do you want me to leave?'

'There's no time like the present,' he told her
cheerfully, now he was sure of her co-operation.
'They want to make quite sure we've got it right
before they optimise the race car for Estoril.'

'What's the problem—do you know?'

'If it isn't the drivers, you mean!' he laughed. 'No,
seriously, they're worried the volatility might be too
high. That's why they're at Paul Ricard. Fluke
weather conditions up from Africa, so the circuit was
thirty-two degrees yesterday afternoon.'

'But it's early October!' Kate protested.

'Mmm, hard to believe, isn't it? Anyway that's
why they're there. Take thin clothes, Kate, I gather
it's pretty humid as well. . . Still, it's good practice
for what lies ahead, I suppose.'

'Flights?' Kate queried as she handed over her
notes.

'All taken care of. Can you make your own way to
Heathrow? Check-in time eighteen-thirty.'

'You don't believe in giving a girl much time, do
you?'

'Not such an organised girl as our Dr Kate!'
She wished she weren't so aware of the sarcasm
that lay behind his words. 'You can catch up on
the reading in-flight. Here are your tickets. Don't
lose them or your passport. And——' he gave her
a speculative smile '—try to enjoy yourself!

You know the expression about all work and no play?'

'You'd be the first to complain if I so forgot myself,' she laughed back at him, 'but you needn't worry. I'll cope and try not to damage too many egos in the process.'

'Clever girl!' he smiled. 'All the same, it would do you good to relax a bit. There's no need to bite everyone's head off just because they notice you're a woman.'

Kate couldn't stop the tide of colour that swept her pale cheeks. 'Er—well, thanks. . .' Unwilling to prolong the conversation in case it took an even more embarrassing turn, she said her goodbyes.

'Keep in touch, Kate!'

'I will.' She took the folder he handed her and made her escape.

It didn't take her long to pack the few clothes she would need, even though her mind was far away in the past. Quietly, competently, she shut up her flat before making her way to the Underground to catch the tube to Heathrow.

She was Dr Katharine Ash, twenty-five years old, able to handle the admiration she got from the opposite sex with aplomb, supremely confident of her destiny. Navy cotton culottes were teamed with the soft centre of an avocado-green shirt and a navy jacket, long and loosely fitted. Sheer stockings showed off her long legs, and the whole outfit was finished off with low-heeled navy shoes. Suitable, smart, the effect was an outward expression of the carefully constructed façade she showed the world.

Why did she feel then that the whole edifice was about to crumble and fall down, leaving her exposed and defenceless?

None of this showed on her face, but a certain rigidity of jaw would have betrayed to the careful watcher that perhaps she wasn't quite as calm and in control as she wished to appear.

Later on the flight to Nice Kate let herself regress ten years to relive once more her beloved only brother's funeral, something she had forbidden herself to do ever since she'd left home to go to university.

The images were still as clear as the rain that had fallen so dispiritedly on the mourners as they stood at one side of the grave while the rector had intoned the fateful words. 'Earth to earth, ashes to ashes, dust to dust. . .' Her accusing eyes had been fixed on the solitary figure who'd stood a little apart from the others, as if not sure of his right to be there. The intense blue of his eyes had dimmed as he looked up and held her gaze. Once more her tummy contracted in memory. With pain? With pleasure? She still, after all these years, did not know, and one hand clenched in involuntary anguish at what she thought of as her intolerable betrayal of her brother.

In a few hours she would come face to face once more with that same man who was responsible for his death and this time she was intent on making absolutely sure that what had been a teenage crush on her part remained just that. Something she'd suffered, like chickenpox: nasty, but with few if any lasting effects. A thing to be forgotten, and certainly not something that had any power in the present except that of a distant unhappy memory.

Ace Barton, world champion and on present form looking likely to make it a second time. Charismatic, charming, he'd become a national hero. He was a darling of the Press—it seemed he could do little wrong. Kate found it hard to avoid hearing about him; he seemed daily to be permeating her senses almost as if he were personally hounding her even though she accepted that had to be crazy thinking on her part.

Motor racing had featured on the periphery of her life as far back as she could remember. Her father had been the successful owner of a chain of garages who in his youth had also raced. When her brother had looked likely to become a chip off the old block, he'd been given all the support of a loving father intent on realising his own dreams through his son.

Eddie's death had been a nightmare that had haunted her family for the last ten years. Neither father and mother, nor sister, had ever been able to talk about it, either between themselves or with outsiders. Kate knew that the wound was still as raw and bleeding in her parents' mind as her own.

It was inevitable therefore that she should have looked for a career in motor racing—at least that was what she told herself. It had nothing to do with the fact that Ace Barton's hard-won road to the top just proved to her how ruthless he must have been to have attained his ultimate goal. It was just pure chance that her job as a fuel technician would ensure that their paths would eventually cross, wasn't it? If she found it stretching credulity that a meeting between them wasn't inevitable she'd always fiercely denied to herself that she had any interest in seeing him again, so why should she be feeling so shivery and hot, almost as if she had a fever?

All in all she got herself in such a state that it was a distinct let-down when she was met by Mike Booker, the team manager, although why she should have thought that the reigning world champion would bother to come and meet a flight at Nice airport was a question she wasn't too happy to answer.

'Hi! It's good to meet you at last. We've all heard a great deal about you!'

'You have?' she responded, still somewhat in a daze.

'Absolutely. You're the toast of the IMP back-room boys, and now I can see why!' Kate tried to ignore his admiring glance, but she couldn't help blushing a little, which showed how much off balance she was because normally she was so used to this sort of conversation that she could, as it were, verbally handle it with one hand tied behind her back.

It took a fierce effort to get her back on her mental feet. 'That's very kind of you, but you ought to remember that there's no competition to speak of back in the laboratory!' She dismissed his admiring look with a cool smile in exchange.

There was a good deal of curiosity behind Mike's admiration, but he managed to curtail it until they were in the car. 'What on earth induced you to become anything so esoteric as a fuel technician?' he demanded.

'Esoteric?' she queried. 'Surely not.'

'Definitely esoteric when a girl looks like you! Why, you could have had a career in modelling or something. . .'

Kate smiled sweetly as she saw his eyes probing the possibilities of her figure. 'Not modelling. . .' She deliberately let a little silence grow between them. 'I'm rather too well-endowed for that particular career.'

'You can say that again!' He seemed to be having great difficulty in keeping his eyes on the road, but after a corner entailed leaving rather a lot of tyre on the road he apologised then grinned at her. 'Sorry about that!'

Kate, having been swung hard against the passenger door, wasn't best pleased. 'You'd do better to look where we're going,' she snapped, 'rather than trying to work out my vital statistics!'

'Yes, ma'am!' He gave her a salute, but didn't appear to be too chastened. 'Anyway, you haven't answered my question. Why did you choose to become a fuel technician?'

'Why not?' She shrugged her shoulders. 'I got my chemistry degree and like everybody else I applied for whatever jobs were going at the time. I like working in a team, and this seemed an interesting career. My father owned garages, so cars have always been a big part of my life.'

'Even so —— ' he shot her another curious look before concentrating again on his driving ' — I'm sure there were plenty of other openings in careers more obviously suited to a woman.'

She swung her hair back from her face impatiently, aware of the heat of the evening even though the car they were travelling in was air-conditioned. 'Look, I'm not a feminist as such but I have to admit I rather resent that remark! Why shouldn't I find it interesting to work with fuels? Even you must admit that it's become an exciting and extremely important job over the last few years, certainly as far as Carlisle Flint is concerned!'

'OK, OK. . .' He lifted both hands off the steering-wheel momentarily. 'I didn't intend to stand on your corns!'

Kate gave a big sigh. 'If you knew how bored I get trying to answer that same question. . .'

He gave a rueful laugh. 'I'm sorry, I should have thought of that. Anyway your colleagues have a high opinion of your skills.'

She turned to him with the first real interest in her face that he'd seen. 'You've been having problems?' she enquired delicately. Mike sighed and gave up, for the moment at least, trying to turn the conversation into channels other than work.

'You could say that. . .' he began cautiously, and after that Kate ensured the conversation stayed firmly on business rails until they arrived at the hotel which the team used when testing in the south of France. She refused Mike's offer of a drink in the bar before going to her room, saying she preferred to meet the rest of the team in the morning.

Mike let her go with rueful amusement in his dark

eyes as she made her way towards the lift, having refused all offers of help with her overnight bag, which she slung over one shoulder. It was a pity that he turned away to join the others in the bar when he did, otherwise he might have seen that Kate appeared to change her mind about something and was returning towards the small reception desk.

In fact she was just checking up on room service, wondering if it was too late to order a plain omelette and salad in her room. She'd refused the airline food, and now found herself ravenously hungry.

Five minutes later she was sitting at a small table at the back of the dining-room, hidden from but within full hearing of the noisy bar. A glass of dry white wine was brought to her, and as she sipped it, trying to relax her tense muscles, she heard Mike's voice rising above a roar of protest.

'She's gone to bed! She says she's tired!'

There were several rude noises and, 'Tell that to the marines!' quite apart from other suggestive remarks, before the noise subsided.

'Come on, Mike, tell us what she looks like? Is she really as good as the lab boys say?'

'I'd say she looks pretty good by any standards myself, but watch it, chaps! There's a large "keep out" sign.'

'You mean she wasn't interested in your middle-aged charms?' There was a roar of laughter.

'I have to admit that she didn't seem overly impressed!' was the good-natured response.

Kate felt her cheeks tinge once more with pink as she went on listening to the good-natured chaff Mike

Booker was taking on her behalf. Her omelette appeared with commendable rapidity, flanked by a green salad and some freshly cut French bread.

She wasted little time in starting to eat, her quick brain turning over alternative scenarios as she debated whether to show herself to the Carlisle Flint team, or disappear quietly to her room. On balance she thought it would be more fun to show herself, and let them know she'd overheard their conversation. That way she'd be more in command of the situation instead of turning up the next morning knowing all eyes were going to be fixed on her.

The excitement that was building up inside her had nothing to do with the fact that Ace Barton was probably just a few feet away from her, she told herself as she tried desperately hard to try and disentangle from the different voices one she hoped to recognise. She cleaned her plate in the time-honoured way with a piece of bread, then summoned the waiter to inform him she'd have her coffee next door.

She stood up and walked over to the arch that separated the two rooms, taking her time to search the room for Mike. That wasn't difficult, because he was sitting in the middle of the largest and noisiest group in the room—also they were the only ones speaking English. She was full of tension as her eyes searched the group with seeming casualness. Her body went momentarily slack with relief, or was it disappointment? Ace Barton was not there.

There weren't any wolf-whistles but the sudden silence that greeted her appearance in the archway

brought a rueful tilt to her lips as she gently raised
her eyebrows until her eyes met the disconcerted
ones of the team manager.

'Hi!' She moved forward gracefully. 'I decided not
to go to my room after all. Do you mind if I join you
with my coffee?' Dino Tremiti, the number-two
driver, was sitting next to Mike, his eyes amused as
he gave her a very comprehensive survey.

'Kate — er — Dr Ash I mean. . .' Mike stood up,
his face making it quite clear he wondered how much
she had overheard.

'Kate will do nicely.' She smiled at him, and the
others, and as the waiter appeared at her side with
her coffee she was amused to see the speed at which
twenty men were on their feet offering her a chair.
The waiter placed her coffee down on one of the
small tables with a flourish, then whisked another
chair from an empty table to make up the numbers.

'*Voilà, mademoiselle*!'

She sat down next to Mike, who started to introduce her to everybody. 'Of course we're not all here,
but you've now met most of the team.'

Kate smiled and gave a general, 'Hi.' There were
really too many people for individual greetings.

'Er — when did you come downstairs, Kate?' Mike
demanded.

'I never went to my room!' She gave him a kind
smile. 'I've just had an omelette and salad in the
dining-room.' She gestured casually with her hand.

'Oh my God!' she heard Mike mutter under his
breath, and she laughed at his discomfort.

'I gathered you all wanted to meet me, so it

seemed a bit unkind to make you wait until the following morning. . .'

'You heard us?' Dino leant forward, his brown eyes laughing.

'I heard you. . .'

'And you forgive us?' Mike interjected.

'What was there that I could possibly object to?' she countered smoothly. 'I just hope that after that build-up I've lived up to my reputation!'

'*Bellissima*!' Dino stood up then took her hand and kissed it, his dark eyes all the time holding hers as they laughed back at her. 'But how could you doubt it? I know I speak for all of us. . .' She couldn't help laughing back at him, and when the others saw that she was genuinely amused they relaxed. Once they were over the shock she was accepted as being a decorative new addition to the team. Naturally it wasn't long before they were all talking shop, although she was amused to note that they were discreet, confining their comments to generalities rather than specifics as they were in a public place.

Because the team were only testing she was, once again, the only woman around. None of the PR girls or secretaries who would be in evidence on race days was there. This was purely business, and for all the jolly camaraderie Kate was aware that most of the men she'd met this evening had grave reservations about her ability to do her job well now that they'd seen her.

In their eyes she was just too glamorous to be serious about her job and Kate realised she was going to have her work cut out tomorrow morning if she was to get and retain their respect on equal terms. It was the thought of this that had her standing up after about half an hour in preparation to go to her room. She addressed her comments to Mike.

'I shall want to be down at the track early tomorrow morning. Is there anyone who'll drive me?'

'I shall do it myself,' he answered.

'Good! I shall need to see today's print-outs and talk to the drivers tomorrow,' she followed up firmly.

'They'll be there, but if you want to make a start on the print-outs I can let you have some tonight?' She gave him a nod of agreement. 'Why don't you order breakfast in your room and we'll be ready to leave at eight tomorrow morning?'

'That sounds fine by me.' She smiled a general goodnight to everyone and started to walk away, accompanied by Mike. He waited until they were out in Reception before apologising again about what she must have overheard while she was eating her supper.

'Forget it, Mike. I've been working in a male environment now for several years, and I've got quite used to hearing my colleagues speculate about me and my private life! It's only likely to cause a problem if they think my work isn't going to be up to standard. You might just remind your team that I wouldn't be working with IMP if they didn't think I was up to the job. Blend Six that you've been trying out here is pretty much my baby, although everything really is a team effort, but that's why Jason has sent me out here to deal with it.'

There was respect in the older man's eyes as he looked at her. 'I see you're one step ahead of us all down the line! OK, I'll pass on your message. By the way, you needn't worry that any of them will bother you unduly. . .'

Kate raised her brows. 'I wasn't worried. I'm quite capable of handling problems in that area!' she snapped back. She was instantly aware that she'd over-reacted as she saw the expression on his face.

'I'm sorry,' she apologised a little stiffly, 'but really I don't expect to be treated with kid gloves. Try to forget that I'm a woman, and there should be no problems!'

'That will be a little difficult,' he agreed politely, 'but I'll do my best and pass your feelings on to the rest of the team. Goodnight.' With old-fashioned politeness he carried her bag to the lifts then walked away. She was left feeling uncomfortably in the wrong, as if by trying to deny her femininity she'd somehow denigrated herself.

As she stepped out on to the third floor, her dark brows were drawn together in the beginnings of a frown because she was still thinking of that last conversation. The hotel wasn't really big enough for her to get confused as she checked up whether to turn left or right down the passage.

Because she was tired, she fumbled slightly as she tried to get the key to turn in the lock.

'You look as if you could do with a bit of help. . .' The familiar voice froze her into unaccustomed rigidity. Helplessly she watched him remove the key from her nerveless fingers and insert it into the lock where it turned easily, clicking the door open. 'There you go, no problem!'

A practised smile was on her lips but his eyes had moved rapidly, assessingly over her figure until their appreciation eventually showed on his face. 'I don't think we've met?' There was just the faintest trace of hesitation behind his smooth approach, as if for once he wasn't quite sure that was true.

Kate, humiliated at being so totally forgotten, tried to deny her pleasure at being the recipient of his undoubted interest but was undecided about what to answer. No doubt his physical closeness didn't help her to think clearly because he was more breath-takingly sexy than he had been as a young man. Now, in his early thirties, he was surrounded by an aura of such vital confidence that she was sure it attracted a positive response from anyone within his orbit. The blue eyes were surrounded now by small laughter-lines, but that added to his attraction, and the dark eyebrows were as mobile as she remembered.

Thick dark hair begged to have fingers run through it, but the wide mouth was still dominated by the thickness of his lower lip, which gave his face such potent sexuality.

If he didn't remember her why should she tell him who she was? He was looking at her with faint amusement in his eyes, one eyebrow slightly raised, and she became aware that he was quite used to this reaction from women to his undoubted charisma. This thought, combined with the hurt of his having forgotten her family so completely, helped her to remain calm.

'No, we haven't met,' she lied. 'Thank you for your help, although it wasn't strictly necessary.' Her voice was firm and dismissive, and as she saw the beginnings of surprise on his face at her rejection she moved swiftly into her room and started to close the door. With any other man she would have succeeded, but Ace had the lightning-quick reactions of a top racing driver. Before she could quite close the door, his foot was in the jamb.

'Hey, wait a minute!' he protested. 'I was only trying to say "hello" and introduce myself.'

Kate pulled the door back a few inches. 'Hello, Ace Barton! And you've no need to introduce yourself, as I'm sure you're all too aware! Now I would be grateful if you would remove your foot from my door.'

The foot remained firmly in place. 'But you haven't told me your name!' he protested, the blue eyes now dancing with amusement as he took in her affronted expression.

'I'm afraid you'll have to be content with just knowing my room number!' she snapped. 'Now, if you don't want me to call the manager and make a fuss, remove your foot!'

'Only if you promise to have lunch with me tomorrow!' he demanded outrageously.

Kate's brows rose slowly. So, he'd been planning on cutting the test sessions short, had he? He was the one who'd complained the most loudly and vociferously about Blend Six not being up to the job, that the burn characteristics were wrong, that the car was running uneven.

'Yes, I'll certainly have lunch with you. Where are you testing — Paul Ricard?' She was slightly amused to see a disconcerted expression on his face, also disappointment at her too prompt acceptance. She guessed he must get tired of his easy conquests. His slow nod of agreement was enough. 'Good. I'll meet you there, then, say about one o'clock?'

He swallowed briefly, and Kate was aware that he was already regretting his rash invitation. Without wasting time, she managed to close the door, having noticed that he'd removed his foot the minute he'd become a little uncomfortable. She waited silently behind the door, her face flushed, half excited, half disappointed that he didn't take it further by knocking for admittance, until she came to her senses. How could he pursue her further if he didn't even know her name?

As she slowly started to unpack and get ready for bed, she thought it was going to be amusing to see his face when he found out exactly who she was tomorrow. She was grateful for the air-conditioning, because she was quite well aware that her unruly emotions were going to make it difficult for her to sleep.

When her alarm woke her up the next morning, she felt heavy-eyed and lacking in energy, but that was probably because her sleep had been long in coming and had been plagued with dreams when she had eventually managed to drop off.

A cool shower managed to sharpen her up to normal. Working clothes today were olive-green Bermuda shorts, a matching T-shirt with the IMP

logo front and back, and trainers over thin green
cotton socks, leaving her long legs bare. The weather
looked heavy and thundery, as if the unseasonable
warmth would soon break. Her hair was in a simple
pony-tail, and she pulled out a cotton peaked cap in
the team colours for wearing on the track.

Breakfast had been fruit and coffee; she'd firmly
resisted the croissants with butter and apricot jam.
Mike was waiting for her in the lobby when she came
down, and she was pleased to see that he too had
dressed as informally as possible in deference to the
humidity. Today their conversation was solely work,
and both seemed happy to keep it so as they made
their way to the circuit.

Once there Kate was too busy immersing herself
in her work to worry about Ace in the pits. There
was too much information which she had to read,
process, then come to a conclusion about before she
was ready to change the blend they were using.

They weren't going to run the cars until midday
when the heavy heat really built up. Kate knew all
too well that hot weather problems were greatly
influenced by the design of the fuel system, but fuel
volatility and atmospheric pressure were also important. The result could be engine roughness during
acceleration, loss of power, and, in some cases,
stalling.

Some of those problems had already shown up on
the print-outs, let alone from the drivers. The time
was coming when she'd have to see for herself. While
the mechanics were setting up the cars, she thought
she'd go outside into one of the empty stands to try

to find a breath of wind, anything rather than standing in the back of the pits in the high humidity which made her skin glow.

Holding her notes like a fan, she walked slowly out into the open, but the heavy heat from the leaden sky soon drove her back into the shade. Just for a moment she began to be sorry for Ace Barton. Dressed up in his fireproof overalls, he was certainly going to earn some of the millions he made this morning.

A hand took hold of her wrist. 'What the hell are you doing here? How the hell did you get past security?'

Think of the devil, she told herself lightly, trying to play down the effect his nearness had on her. 'Don't be silly——!' she started to say, but he didn't wait for her to finish.

'This is not the time or the place for a pit-popsy, sweetheart. So you got my note crying off and thought you'd come and try to change my mind?'

Kate didn't like the cynical look on his face. 'Let go of me,' she demanded loudly, 'or I'll call——'

Once more he interrupted. 'For help?' His blue eyes narrowed as he took in her curves. 'You might think you look great, but you don't fool me. What are you—a journalist? Or spying for the opposition?'

'Neither, you idiot!' He let go of her as Mike joined them, giving her a curious look. 'Will you explain to your driver,' she yelled furiously, 'that I'm the fuel technician from IMP and not some stupid little blonde who can't wait to get to know him better?'

Mike took one look at her furious face, and Ace's flabbergasted one, and put up a hand to hide his mouth, but he couldn't stop his eyes from dancing with amusement.

'Ace! Meet Dr Kate Ash, the representative from IMP whom I'm sure you've heard about!'

CHAPTER TWO

AT THE end of a long and exhausting working day Kate retired to her room with one thing only on her mind, and that was a need for a cool shower. The weather was still heavy and sultry, the promised storm still not having broken.

Both she and Ace had kept their inevitable contact strictly business; in fact she had to be impressed with his total single-mindedness with his job, finding in his perfectionist attitude an answering chord within herself. She also had been able to put her feelings on hold as she concentrated on the problems facing her. All the same, she wasn't best pleased to be disturbed by a knock on her door as she wrapped herself in a towelling robe and hid her wet hair in a turban after she stepped out of the shower.

She opened it impatiently. 'Yes?' she queried, cross at being interrupted, but her expression changed when she saw Ace standing outside. She hoped her face hadn't betrayed those inner feelings that had leapt into unwelcome life at the sight of him. 'Oh, it's you! Well, you'd better come in, unless you'd rather wait until I'm dressed?'

Her attempt at sarcasm was wasted as she took in his grim expression. Good heavens, surely he wasn't uptight because she hadn't told him who she was this morning?

27

He stepped past her into the room, then turned to face her, his face set in uncompromising lines. 'You're Eddie Ash's sister, aren't you? Why did you lie and say you hadn't met me before?'

Kate's face went as white as the towel around her head. 'It wasn't really a lie. You'd only seen me a couple of times, and then you weren't exactly falling over yourself to speak to me!' she spat back.

'You were a fifteen-year-old kid!' he answered. 'What the hell did you expect, that I should treat you as some kind of equal? When you came to those two meetings at Oulton Park you were wearing school uniform!'

She was shocked by the accuracy of his memory. 'How can you remember that so clearly?' she whispered.

His words and voice spun her instantly back into the past. She was a tall, awkward-looking girl overwhelmed at being close to someone who had long been her idol. She had blushed a fiery red as he had walked over, dressed in his race gear, to talk to her brother. Eddie had introduced them casually.

'You've never met my sister Kate, have you?'

'No. . .' Blue eyes had flickered over her politely but with a definite lack of interest. 'Hi, Kate!' He'd shaken her hand.

Eddie had grinned. 'She's a fan, Ace. You'll have to give her a kiss!'

Ace had looked at her scarlet face and his eyes were amused. 'You're sure it isn't catching?' he'd teased, once more looking at her red face.

Poor Kate had never been given a chance to

answer. A pretty girl had run up to him and thrown her arms around his neck before kissing him passionately.

'Good luck!' she had breathed, before calmly walking away.

Kate had noticed that Ace now had a small piece of paper clutched in his hand, something that definitely hadn't been there before. His attention had been fiercely concentrated on the back of the girl as she had slowly walked away, his blue eyes narrowed in appreciation.

Humiliated, she'd crept away, knowing that her brother too had been interested in the unknown girl.

'I have near-photographic recall,' he sneered, and Kate blinked, immediately brought back to the present. 'It's one of the things that has helped me to become world champion. I can remember every track I've ever raced on, every bump, every turn. . .'

Kate had regained her cool, but her expression was wary. 'So?' The memory of her brother, his laughing brown eyes and wide smile, lowered the temperature between them even further.

'Do you and your family think I'm responsible for his death?' The blue eyes were cold and watchful as he lounged casually in front of her, the thin sea island cotton shirt allowing the darker hairs on his chest to show through. His jeans were tight-fitting, showing off his compact figure.

The shock of his words had her narrowing her eyes as her heart began to beat uncomfortably fast in her chest. She was aware of danger, yet wasn't quite sure from what quarter the threat came, so she compromised.

'We've never discussed it,' she answered coldly, knowing the truth would sound totally unbelievable. Eddie's death had changed so much. Afterwards her home had become a place of coldness, of ugly, hidden, unspoken emotions.

He looked his disgust. 'Oh, come on! You can't expect me to believe that!'

'I can assure you that it's the truth.' Maybe it was the flat calm, almost dead timbre of her voice that helped convince him, because a heavy frown made him look angry.

'That's sick! Do you mean to tell me your mother and father never discussed that last accident with you?'

She shook her head. 'No. They—I——' She broke off, trying to regain her cool. This was awful. How could she explain that she'd been too frightened of the dammed-up emotion she'd felt in both her mother and father? That if she'd triggered it by asking questions she might be drowned in the flood of pain that would be released? She made herself stand a little taller. 'Really, I can't see what my family has to do with you now! Eddie was killed ten years ago.'

She wished she felt as sure of herself as the man so casually lounging opposite her.

'I'll tell you, sweetheart! I don't want a fuel technician who could be full of bitter thoughts of revenge having anything to do with my car! I'm going to recommend to IMP that you're sent back to the laboratory and they send us someone we know and trust! There's too much running on these last end-of-season races for me to be prepared to take a chance on you!'

The shock of his words pulled her up short, her intelligence at last alerted to the source of danger. Desperately she reminded herself that she was Eddie's sister and prayed for courage.

'Ace Barton running scared?' It was one of the hardest battles of her life to drop that remark lightly into the charged atmosphere between them. 'Now why should you think I would be harbouring thoughts of revenge, unless. . .' she let a silence grow '. . .you know a very good reason why I should feel that way?'

'Damn you! I might have guessed you'd make trouble just by looking at you.'

'Really? That wasn't the impression I got last night.'

'That little mistake was corrected when you got my note this morning, as you know very well!'

Kate raised her eyebrows. 'I received no note from you this morning, or any other time!'

'Don't strain my credulity again!' She couldn't help the tinge of pink that flooded her cheeks at his expression as those blue eyes studied her with contempt.

'Well, if you didn't put it under my door yourself, maybe you'd better just check with Reception downstairs.' Her remote yet detached look seemed to make him uncomfortable.

This time it was his turn for a dull flush to warm the tan on his cheeks. 'So OK you didn't get the note; maybe you didn't need to. You knew before you shut your door in my face last night that I was having second thoughts!'

'I'm flattered that you think I can read your mind,' she told him sarcastically, 'but I can promise you I wasn't sufficiently interested in the outcome to try. I knew perfectly well that we'd be working together today.'

'Yes, that was a dirty trick on your part, wasn't it?'

She smiled at him, before turning away. 'If you say so. . .' She shrugged her shoulders, her uninterest eloquent. 'Now if you don't mind I'd rather be left alone to finish drying my hair.'

'I mean it, Kate! I'm not going to tolerate you working on this team with me.'

'I think you're going to have to, Ace!' There was a purposeful look now in her eyes that gave him pause. 'I don't think it would be very wise of you to try and get me sent back to London.'

'Oh, why?' This time it was his eyes that were narrowed as he watched her as closely as any cat after a mouse.

'Because if you try to do anything so misguided I might have to give a Press interview to explain just why I got under your skin so badly!'

His face closed up completely at her words, almost as if he was wearing a mask. 'You really do think I was responsible for Eddie's death, don't you?'

'Since you ask, then yes. . .'

There was a nasty silence and Kate felt that the

atmosphere was now so heavy with unspoken words thta it could be cut with a knife.

'Are you planning to avenge his death?' he enquired, neither his voice or face giving anything away.

'Don't be so melodramatic!' Her brows drew together in a formidable frown.

His own rose in simulated surprise. 'What other reason could there be for a girl who looks like you doing your job?'

Kate felt fury well up in her. 'What an arrogant, narrow-thinking man you are!' Her voice was bitter. 'Why should it be so strange for me to find work with IMP? You know perfectly well that my background was always cars, racing ones at that! Why should I be debarred from a career in an area that interests me just because you're a Grand Prix driver?'

'I just wish I could be sure that your chosen career had nothing to do with the fact that it was mine!' His lazy, almost relaxed tone of voice did not disguise his fierce determination to find out what he thought of as the truth.

Kate couldn't stop her face from flaming at the astuteness of his answer, and sought to cover up her confusion in attacking him again. 'Such concern smacks of a guilty conscience to me! All you've said so far just confirms what I have long suspected — that you were so determined to get to the top, so determined to succeed that day, that you quite deliberately drove my brother off the track!'

The silence between them seemed to lengthen interminably, and her nerves were stretched almost unbearably as she waited for his answer. The blue eyes were studying her with an intentness she found exceedingly disconcerting. 'So, you think I am your brother's murderer?' The words came out softly, the very gentleness of their delivery adding to their horror.

Kates cheeks went white, before flaming red. 'No! No, I don't think you thought of murder. I think you were so intent on winning that you didn't care what happened to anyone that got in your way. I don't suppose you thought for one minute that anything really drastic would happen to him. . .'

'So I'm guilty of manslaughter, then?'

Kate swung away, unable to meet his eyes. 'If you say so. . .' She stared unseeing out of the big plate-glass window that looked down on to the hotel's rather undistinguished forecourt.

'Have you never seen the video replay of the accident?' The sarcastic note in his voice had her swinging round furiously to face him again.

'No! I never saw anything, I just heard my father telling my mother——' She broke off abruptly, one hand rising guiltily to her mouth.

'What did your father say?' His voice sounded sharp. She turned away, unable to face him again, her eyes full of unaccustomed tears, but he pulled her round till once more she was forced to meet his eyes. 'Tell me!' His hands bit tightly into her arms.

'I didn't hear much! It was just the end of a conversation. . .'

'Tell me!' His hands increased their grip painfully.

'He said. . .he said if anyone was to blame for

Eddie's death it was you!' His hands dropped sharply away, and she put up her own hands to rub the skin were his fingers had marked her.

'That's great!' he laughed sharply. 'What hypocrites your family are! He was the one who was responsible for your brother's death, as everyone in the business knew!'

'What do you mean?' Kate looked at him, her hurt and bewilderment written large on her face.

'Your father pushed his son to succeed where he had failed. He never took into account that Eddie didn't really want to make a career as a racing driver——'

'That's a lie!' Kate interrupted, her eyes now full of tears. 'He loved to race, he told me so. . .'

'In the beginning, yes, he did, but he didn't want to be pushed out of his class. He knew he was never going to be good enough for Formula One but his father wouldn't listen. He wanted his son to be a champion, and he did everything he could to force him to go on racing against his better judgement!'

'How do you know all this?'

'Because he was my friend, and we talked. I knew he wanted to get out, but your father always managed to persuade him to do just one more race. Eddie tried hard to get your father to sponsor me, but he wasn't interested. It had to be his son.' Kate's quick ears picked up the remembered bitterness. So, Ace had hoped her father would do something for him?

'What really happened that day, then?' Kate could

hardly fail to be aware that Ace was now reliving the past.

'He was bloody terrified. I knew it, and the mechanics knew it. He'd had that spin-out in practice and he didn't like the way the car was handling. He didn't want to race but your father insisted he take his place on the grid. It was the semi-finals of the Formula Three and we were all going for it, trying to make sure of a place in the final line-up.

'We came together because it looked as if he was going to try to take my line to the corner. I didn't shut the door on him, I left it as long as I dared, but he was going so fast he hadn't a hope. He clipped me and spun off into the wall and broke his neck.' He shut his eyes for a moment, but not before Kate had seen a flicker of private anguish. 'You can check with whoever you like but I was totally exonerated of any blame at the time, and I resent you and your family's implications that I was responsible for Eddie's death! The blue eyes were lit with a fierce conviction as they met hers.

'You mention your doubts to anyone outside this room and I'll sue you and your family for everything they've got!'

Kate looked back at him consideringly, trying hard not to feel intimidated by the fierce energy that was being directed at her. 'It's your word against my father's, then. . .'

Ace smiled, but it didn't reach his eyes. 'I suggest you look at the evidence with your own eyes before you start accusations that you might find impossible to back up. I have a copy of the race tape back at my

flat in London. Why don't you come round one
evening soon and look at it?' He ignored her wince
of protest. 'It's been ten years. Don't you think by
now you can face it? Also you might consider that
what I've just told you could be the truth.'

Kate knew she would do as he suggested. She'd
already virtually accused him of killing her brother.
However unpleasant she would find it, she would
have to watch Eddie's fatal accident, even if the
thought made her feel ill. It would also entail another
meeting between them, a small voice inside told her,
shocking her with its message.

Try as she might, Kate found it impossible to be
completely unaware of the sexual magnetism of the
man. Furious as he undoubtedly was with her, she
still felt a thrill to be so close to him. She turned
away, pretending indifference. 'All right, I'll meet
you in London. When?' she finished bluntly.

'Give me your phone number and I'll call you. I'm
not too sure of my immediate plans. When are you
returning?'

'Hopefully tomorrow, unless you manage to find
something else to complain about in our
department.'

'I think that's unlikely after today. . .' He gave her
a look of grudging admiration. 'I suppose I have to
admit that you're good at your job.'

'I'm just a small part of a team, so you needn't get
your knickers in a twist trying to be polite!' she
snapped.

'OK, OK. . .' He looked surprised.

'Now if you don't mind I'd like to have my room to myself so I can finish dressing.'

This time there was no denying the speculative gleam in his eye as he studied her figure through the folds of the towelling robe.

'Are you a natural blonde?' he queried. 'I don't remember you being quite so fair as a teenager!'

'Mind your own business!' she replied stiffly.

'Why be so stuffy?' This time he gave her a genuine smile. 'Your colouring is so unusual that I'd have thought you'd have got quite used to answering that question by now!'

'Would you?' She walked across to the door and opened it. 'On your way, Ace Barton. Don't forget I'm not one of your fans.'

A dark colour swept across his face. 'If you weren't Eddie's kid sister I'd have given you a far harder ride for what you've just accused me of this evening, so don't push your luck, Dr Kate Ash, because you might come to regret it!' He stopped by the door. 'You're forgetting something, sweetheart!'

Kate's heart, which had been beating uncomfortably fast at his proximity, slowed down at his expression of dislike. 'What have I forgotten?' she demanded aggressively.

'Your phone number, remember?'

Cross at being caught out, she moved over to the dressing-table to find some paper, then wrote down the number of her London flat.

'I'm normally at home most evenings,' she told him, trying to ignore his disbelieving look as she handed it over.

'What a waste, but then I suppose I'm not too surprised,' he drawled.

Kate was quite unable to resist rising to his bait although she knew it was madness. 'What do you mean?'

There was a cruel smile on his mouth as once more he gave her a comprehensive survey. 'I bet you've never had a real boyfriend in your life, have you? In spite of your good looks you put men off once they try to get close to you. You remind me of a beautiful ripe peach just waiting to be picked but when you're opened up—surprise, surprise! You're all old and shrivelled inside. There's no heart, no life in you; you're like a cardboard cut-out and you want to work on it, Kate, because you're not getting any younger, are you? Soon it'll be too late and all that emptiness will start to show.' He slipped out, pulling the door closed behind him, leaving her cruelly defenceless against his bitter attack.

The terrifying thing was that he was right about her. She always did choke off any men who showed signs of wanting to get close to her and she didn't know why she behaved like that. She was twenty-five years old and still a virgin, and as she looked at her image in the mirror great tears welled up and spilled over as she relived Ace's words. She was only half alive, an empty shell who'd sought to hide her deficiencies by becoming a part of a team, but it hadn't worked.

She remembered her father's words after he'd blamed Ace for his son's death; words she'd never repeated to anybody. 'If I had to have only two children, then why the hell did I have to lose my only son?' Her father's anguish, as he'd shouted those words at her mother, had pierced her to the quick, her mother's shushing noises hardly heard as she'd crept away to her room to hide. That was when she'd first decided to try to make up to her father for what he'd lost.

Kate returned to her job in London with her armour firmly in place, and if, for the first time, she was conscious of an emptiness in her life that her job wasn't going to be able to satisfy she refused to accept it.

Ace called the second night after she got back. 'Kate? Can you come round here tomorrow evening? I'm sorry it's such short notice, but that's the best I can do.' He gave her his address.

She tried fiercely to control the sudden rush of pleasure that hearing his voice again so soon gave her. 'That'll be fine. What time do you want me to come around?'

Her heart sank as he answered, 'Make it soon after work, will you? I've got a dinner date I don't want to cut, and this shouldn't take long.'

Acute disappointment had her dropping the phone without even acknowledging his last explanation. Why had she set out to antagonise, to accuse him of her brother's death? Whom was she really punishing by behaving this way? Him or herself? She didn't even know what to believe any more. He'd sounded so sure. She knew that he had been Eddie's best friend—that was why she'd always found it so hard

to accept that he could have deliberately driven her
brother off the track. Why was her father so sure
Ace was to blame?

In a low and antagonistic frame of mind she
accepted that Ace was never going to have any time
for her. That had to be a good thing as far as she was
concerned, she told herself, so therefore she took
him exactly at his word. She turned up at his flat not
having bothered to go home and change, more than
a little tired and jaded after an extremely hard
working day.

He answered the door himself, and she was painfully aware that once again his eyes seemed to study
every part of her. Why did he have to do that?
Perhaps it was part of a plan to hurt her, to punish
her, for her unhappy suspicions about him.

'Come in.' He stood aside as she walked past him.
'Leave your coat on that chair, will you?'

Kate quickly shrugged it off herself, not wanting
to give him any chance of coming near her. She
deliberately refused to look at herself in the strategi-
cally placed mirror.

'You look tired. Had a hard day?' The blue eyes
appeared as hard as steel as her brown ones met
them fleetingly.

She shrugged. 'No more so than usual.'

'Try not to make your dislike quite so obvious,
Kate; it's bad manners when you're a guest in my
house!'

She allowed her brows to rise. 'A pretty unwelcome one, as you made more than plain on the
phone, so why should I bother making an effort to

please you?' Something flashed behind those eyes,
but what it was Kate wasn't sure. Probably it was a
spurt of temper at her having dared to answer him
back. She guessed he wouldn't be used to much of
that from her sex. She sighed; what the hell was she
doing trying to speculate what went on behind that
good-looking façade?

'Would you like a drink?'

Kate had followed him into a big sitting-room,
plain, almost spartan in its simplicity. A couple of
very good oriental rugs were pools of subdued colour
on the polished wood floor. The big windows were
topped by heavy wood poles from which curtains in
raw linen hung, their stunning simplicity at one with
the plain cream-washed walls.

Two enormous sofas in a deep burgundy brocade
looked hugely luxurious in contrast to the rest of the
room as they faced each other across a low glass
table. One end of the room was entirely taken up by
built-in cupboards full of books, photographs and
racing trophies prominently displayed. One of the
largest televisions Kate had ever seen dominated one
side of the room, its VCR with a cassette just waiting
to play. Kate felt sick as she looked at it. Could she
bear to go through with this? She certainly needed
something strong to steady her nerves.

'Thank you. I'll have a brandy.'

'Are you sure?' Ace turned to give her a strange
look.

'Quite. But put some ginger ale in it if it makes
you feel better.' Her voice was light and dismissive.

She noticed belligerently that he did add ginger ale to the brandy.

'Here.' He handed her a glass full of a bubbling, glowing golden mixture. 'Come and sit.'

She followed him over towards one of the big sofas, careful as she sat to leave as much of a gap between them as possible.

'I don't bite, you know!' he told her, a glint of humour momentarily lighting his face.

'You could have fooled me!' she muttered, and took a hefty swig of her drink as his face once more closed up against her. She felt sad and immensely tired that she was about to see for the first time how Eddie had died. Ace pressed the remote-control button and the room became alive to the sound of highly tuned engines revving up. She had no difficulty in picking out her brother's car second to Ace's pole position, her whole body jerking into a forgotten awareness as she watched the start and the jockeying for position before the first corner.

She'd never known any details; she didn't know if the accident happened early on, or whether she would have to sit for a long time just waiting for the inevitable. Without thinking, she drank deeply from her glass, all the time her eyes riveted on to those early leaders as the brandy burnt its way down her throat.

When the end came it was quick, with no warning. Kate stood up, felt the bile rise up in her throat, before she gagged.

'Here!' A white hankie was thrust out to her and she gratefully held it in front of mouth, her eyes wide with desperate appeal. 'Follow me!' She almost ran out of the room, oblivious to everything except her need to get to a bathroom. Ace threw open a door and she collapsed behind it, just having the nerve to click the bolt before events overtook her.

Spent and trembling once the nasty little interlude was over, she then set about trying to tidy herself up. She longed to clean her teeth, but didn't like to touch anything. This was so obviously Ace's bathroom that she felt uncomfortable. She must get out and go home. He'd made it clear enough after all that he didn't expect her to hang about as he had another date. Her face looked grey, and her eyes were still faintly bloodshot. All in all, she decided, not the prettiest of sights, but then what did it matter now?

Quietly she opened the door, and walked silently back down to the passage towards the hall. She could hear what sounded like Ace talking to someone on the phone as she picked up her coat and shrugged herself into it.

'Where the hell do you think you're going?' The molten anger behind the words had her twisting round in shock to face him.

'I — I'm going home!' she stuttered, uncomfortable at being caught out.

'Without saying "goodbye" or anything like that, I suppose?'

His sarcasm put a faint touch of colour back into her cheeks. 'You told me you had another date — what was the point in my hanging around?'

'What kind of man do you think I am?' he started out furiously. 'Did you think I'd ignore the fact that you were suffering from shock? That after enduring obvious trauma I'd leave you to go home alone? My God! I know I'm no saint but not even I have sunk to quite such depths of villainy—even if you find that hard to believe!' He looked at her, the temper suddenly draining away as he assessed her expression.

'I see the video hasn't convinced you?' There was a deceptive calm in his voice.

'No, I can't honestly say it has,' she agreed, her voice also non-committal.

'It doesn't help that FISA have never held me responsible?'

'No, not really. You're a good enough driver to have made it look like an accident.' Her voice was judicial, but she quailed inwardly at the flare of anger that lit the blue eyes.

'So there's no doubt in your mind that I'm to blame?' She thought he had to be capable of almost super-human control because his voice still sounded calm, almost matter-of-fact.

'Of course there are doubts. If it was that certain you wouldn't have got away with it.'

'Thank you!'

His sarcasm left her unwounded, and she just shrugged. 'May I go home now?'

He appeared to ignore her sarcasm, his brows drawn together in a frown. 'What?'

She repeated her request.

'No, I want you to stay and have supper with me.'

She couldn't resist asking him about his date. 'I thought you were supposed to be going out?'

'No, I cancelled it earlier today.'

'What a mistake, but maybe you can put it right, otherwise you'll have to eat alone,' she finished sweetly.

'No, I think not. . . I rather hoped I wouldn't have to face you with this but thanks to your belief that I'm somehow responsible for Eddie's death you force my hand. Did you know your brother gambled, Kate?' He gave one swift look at her horrified expression before continuing. 'I see you did. I paid off his debts, but unfortunately for you, he insisted that he'd pay me back someday and left me with a considerable number of IOUs. Out of misplaced sympathy for his family I never demanded settlement, but equally I didn't tear them up. . .'

'I don't believe you! If you'd had any IOUs you'd have sent them to my father,' she counter-attacked.

'I hate to prove you wrong.' He put his hand in his jacket and brought out a small package.

Rudely, without waiting for him to hand it to her, she snatched it out of his hand, then anxiously turned over the scrawled papers one by one. Her shoulders sagged in defeat and it became clear to the watching man that she accepted their veracity.

'How much did he borrow?' Her voice sounded husky and a little unsure.

'Nearly thirty thousand pounds.'

She drew in her breath in a sharp hiss.

'I had to sell my share in Moffat Engineering, which lost me my chance to drive for them that year. . .' Kate looked bewildered as she watched the memories of amusement and sadness play over his face. 'Your brother took my place. . .'

'Why did you do it? Why did you lend him all that money?' she demanded fiercely, as if somehow trying to put the blame on to him.

'Because he was my best friend; because I hadn't realised then that he was a compulsive gambler. I'd tried to help him before. I didn't want to accept defeat, to acknowledge that there was nothing I— nor anyone else—could do to help,' Ace replied, and it silenced her for a moment, as perhaps it was meant to do.

'What do you want me to do about these?'

She held the package out in front of her, and he quietly removed it from her grasp.

'I'll tell you over dinner.'

'But I don't want to have dinner with you!' she snapped.

'Bad luck!' There was an unkind expression on his face. 'But in the circumstances I think you'll have to, won't you? Unless you want me to get in touch with your father, that is?'

'No!' she interjected in a hurry. 'No. . . I'll deal with it.'

She couldn't interpret the expression on his face as he looked at her. 'Do you want another drink?'

'No. . .' She fought to contain the nausea his words recalled.

'You'll feel better when you've had something to eat,' he told her callously. 'Let's go!'

'I can't, Ace. I'm filthy. Let me go home.'

'Can't or won't?' he queried grimly, but she just shrugged in defeat.

'OK. I'll drive you home so you can change first.' Kate knew it was no good resisting, so she meekly allowed him to shepherd her out of the flat down to the basement where he kept his car.

They were both silent, busy with their own thoughts, apart from her directions, until he drew up in front of the divided house that contained her tiny flat. She left him to prowl restlessly through the family photographs that were prominently displayed as she first took a shower then dithered over what to wear.

Tight stretch velvet leggings and a violet chenille cable sweater seemed OK. It was cold in London compared to the unnatural steamy heat they'd suffered at the Paul Ricard circuit.

'That was quick!' he said, but his eyes complimented her, which she found disconcerting.

'Yes, well, I wasn't going to keep you waiting too long,' she responded.

'Right, let's go!'

He took her to a rather smart Italian restaurant full of intimate little tables far too close together for private conversation. At first Kate was frightened about what they'd find to talk about, but she needn't have worried. By tacit consent they kept their conversation to motor racing, and as Kate knew a surprising amount about automotive engineering she was able to hold her own in open discussion with him.

She guessed he found it intriguing to be able to

talk about his consuming interest in the sport with a girl who not only knew what he was talking about, but could actually offer opinions that were interesting.

When he was driving her home he said, 'I don't intend to lose touch with you, Kate.'

She smiled to herself, rather pleased by what she thought of as a compliment. 'You're satisfied I'm not going to sabotage your chances of becoming world champion for the second time?'

'That's why I don't intend to lose touch with you!' He sounded cold and ruthless. 'Does your job give you total satisfaction?'

Cross with herself for being fooled, her answer was short and to the point.

'Yes, it does!'

'What a pity.' He didn't sound in the least sorry, and she held her breath waiting for him to continue. 'I want you to leave IMP and come and work for me!'

'Are you mad?' Kate could hardly believe her ears.

'No. I just intend making sure you stay right under my eye until the end of the season.'

'I wouldn't dream of giving up my job to work for you!'

'You have very little choice, Kate. If you don't I'll get in touch with your father. . .'

'That's blackmail!'

'Ten out of ten. What are you going to do about it?' He sounded totally dispassionate, as if the outcome wasn't important.

'You can't behave like that! Why, I'll go to the police. . .'

'You do that and I'll pursue your father through the courts for every last penny Eddie owed me.'

Somehow she didn't doubt him, and collapsed in defeat. 'All right, you win. . .'

'There's no need to sound quite so despairing. It's quite possible, if you agree, that IMP will release you for six months to work for me. If you play your cards right, your job could still be waiting for you after that.'

'You'll let me go after six months?'

'I'll put it in writing!' he jeered, before leaning over her to open the car door. 'Give me a little time before breaking the news to your boss. That way I might be able to ensure you'll have a job at the end of it all.' She got out, and, after he had waited to see her enter the house, the car roared off into the night.

CHAPTER THREE

ONCE Kate was alone back in her flat, she lay down on her bed and let the mask slip. She didn't try to fight the tears as her mind played and replayed the whole scene of Eddie's last few moments of life. She allowed herself to feel all the pain she'd denied herself for so long. With total lack of inhibitions she rolled face down and, her mouth buried in her pillow, howled like an animal over his death. The torrent of weeping afterwards left her feeling as weak as any new-born, but it had had a cleansing and calming effect.

Eddie had been dead ten long years, a life so abruptly terminated that she had never come to terms with it. She wondered if her fixation with Ace was because in her mind the two of them were inextricably linked. She knew Eddie's gambling had had disastrous consequences for her family, but it had been a terrible shock to discover he had taken so much from his best friend as well.

Could Eddie have run out of that corner deliberately because he couldn't face the consequences of his gambling? Her logical mind accepted this possibility, as it had done countless times before, but she didn't think her brother would ever have considered suicide. Of course it was crazy to recall Ace's theory about her father. . . That had to be a figment of his imagination to justify his own actions.

What about her own feelings as far as he was concerned? Why was she feeling so muddled? She ought to hate him for what he threatened to do, yet inside she felt a treacherous excitement at the fact that he wanted to keep her close. Perhaps he did find her attractive after all? This had been the root of so many of her fantasies about him in the past, fantasies that involved her having power over him.

She fiercely ignored a small internal voice that warned her there was a fat chance of that coming to pass as far as he was concerned. Why, he'd made his feelings more than clear out in France, hadn't he? She just wasn't his type, and anyway she'd no intention of joining the seemingly endless queue of girls happy to be seen in his company.

All the same it was hard to restrain her pleasure when he called her the following evening.

'Hi, Kate, how are you?'

'Fine. . .' She tried to control her feelings and hoped her voice sounded wooden and lifeless.

'If you're not doing anything how about coming out to supper with me?'

'Why?' she demanded ungraciously.

'Because I find being out with you useful. For a start you don't expect me to behave like some sort of stud. Anyway I thought I'd fill you in on my progress with IMP.'

'You can tell me all that over the phone.'

'No.' His voice was uncompromising. 'Wear something dressy, Kate. I've got to take in a promotional drinks party first, and as the Press will be there they'll focus on you like the leeches they are because you'll be a new face.'

'Thanks!' she answered wryly. 'That's hardly my scene. Why don't I meet you later?'

'Kate, I need your co-operation. I'm fed up with being the target for all those unattached girls who fancy that being seen with me will give them a leg-up in their dubious careers! Don't worry, I won't really throw you to the wolves. You'll just have to put up with being labelled as my latest girlfriend!'

'I can't think of anything I'd loathe more!'

'Kate. . . I don't have to remind you, do I?'

'Oh, God! You're a nightmare. . . Anyway I don't own any really glamorous clothes!'

'Then it's about time you did! You must have got something you wear to parties?'

'Well, yes, but I don't think. . .'

'Just wear your hair loose, Kate, that ought to wow them!'

'You're not suggesting I turn up like Lady Godiva? Because if so. . .'

He laughed. 'I'm shocked!' he answered, amusement making his voice sound warm. 'Much as I like the idea, I don't think your parents would be best pleased would they?'

Kate sighed. 'They're not going to be at all happy if they see any photographs of us together.'

'And that worries you?' The sneer in his voice made her lose her temper.

'Yes, of course that worries me! Anybody but an

insensitive idiot like you would be aware of the problem.'

'You needn't lose your cool. Your father's far too self-centred to care what you do. I should have thought you'd have found that out by now.'

'Don't push me too far, Ace!' Kate ground her teeth in helpless rage.

'OK, if that's the way you want it. Maybe it is time you were made to come out of your shell.' His voice sounded casual. 'Right! We'll try to make it an evening to celebrate, then. The Press'll expect that if you're my new girlfriend. See you. . .' He put the phone down, leaving Kate in a combination of rage and panic at having to go out with him again.

As she looked in her cupboard, trying to control her rising temper, she realised she really had been neglecting her wardrobe — well, certain aspects of it, she told herself as she pushed the smart business suits to one side. It didn't take her long to decide she had precisely two choices — well, one, really, because even though it wasn't cold it would look wrong to go out in thin cotton to the sort of party he was talking about.

The little black designer dress had been an impulse buy earlier in the year, and she'd never worn it. Short and slinky smooth, it was completely plain, depending on her own body curves for its effect. With a boat neck it had short sleeves, and Kate bit her lip as she realised it was going to have a pretty powerful impact. She tried to ignore the fact that inside her head two entirely different converstions were going on about Ace, and this dress neatly encapsulated one of them.

After a shower she put it on with a frown, worried that it really was going to live up to her expectations, teamed up with seamed black tights and her new black slingback shoes. She stared at herself in the mirror. With her hair loose, falling from a centre parting, she looked arresting, even eye-catching. If that doesn't make him sit up and take notice. . .one of the voices in her head started to say until she firmly clamped down on it.

Full of cynical amusement, she continued to stare at herself until, inspired, she started to make up her face carefully, emphasising her brown eyes with liner, and smoky eyeshadow, and dusting her high cheekbones with blusher. Her mouth she kept a pale peach, knowing that a stronger colour lipstick wouldn't be right for the effect she wanted to create. Finally she smiled at her image reflected in her mirror, a small bubble of excitement beginning to build inside as she decided whether or not to wear a gilt necklace with a resin pendant by Pellini which she'd found at Liberty.

Deciding it was right, she left it to swing lightly between her breasts as she sprayed herself with Dune, the new Christian Dior fragrance, on her way to answer the doorbell.

Ace's blue eyes narrowed in approval as they leisurely explored her. Kate found it difficult to keep her colour from rising under the enthusiastic appreciation she was being subjected to, and, to try and

break the dangerous spell, she broke into provocative speech.

'I take it I will do?' she queried with a lift of one
eyebrow.

Ace drew a deep breath. 'You can say that again!
Kate, I don't know what you define as glamour, but,
if you don't think this little outfit of yours is going to
get all the boys hot and panting, then you want your
head seen to. You look tremendously sexy. . .' The
blue eyes held a distinctly disturbing message as they
met her brown ones, and Kate became strongly
aware of danger.

She shrugged her shoulders lightly. 'Good! I
haven't worn this dress before, but I'm glad you
think it's OK. . .' His eyes were still lingering on the
curves hidden by the black material that caught and
shimmered in the light as she moved.

'You know perfectly well you look stunning.' His
voice sounded cynical, but then he smiled, almost as
if he understood the look of sudden shock on her
face, as he once more became that unfriendly
stranger who'd been her brother's best friend. 'Have
you got a coat or something? We'd better be on our
way because the sooner we get to the party and do
our duty, then the sooner we can leave.' He held up
the soft peach wool jacket that Kate intended to
wear, but there was a sudden rueful expression on
his face as he met her eyes again. 'You do realise
you're going to get the Press really going when they
see you this evening, don't you? Not to mention the
teams when they see the pictures. . .'

'Don't be silly, Ace!' Kate replied in her most

matter-of-face voice, hoping that it would hide her half-guilty pleasure at his words. 'The photographs will probably be unrecognisable.'

'No chance of that, not with those cheekbones. Anyway, don't you know if you look good in photos?'

'No, I — er — actually no, I don't!' Ace had caught her on the hop again.

He looked down at her incredulously. 'Do you mean to say no one's ever photographed you?'

'No! Well, not since I was a child ——'

'But surely your parents?' he interjected.

'No. . . They were always more involved with Eddie, you see. I was just a girl, so my father was never really interested in me, and my mother — well, she loved my brother too. . .'

'I never did hold much of a brief for your father, but it seems as if your mother wasn't much better!' he said, his voice making clear how lacking in sympathy he found her family.

Furious, she swung her head away, not knowing what to answer. It seemed as if this man would always somehow have the power to strip her of her narrow protective veneer to expose her vulnerability.

It looked as though she couldn't fool him. 'You don't think you're tarred with the same brush, do you?' He gave her a piercing look. 'You and Eddie, well, you're both proof that miracles happen! How else could anyone explain your mystery? With parents like that you should both have turned out monsters!'

This stiffened her backbone. 'Eddie had his faults

as you know very well!' She gave him a resentful
look. 'And you don't know me yet, Ace! By the end
of the evening you might well be accepting that I'm
a fully paid-up flesh-eating dinosaur like my parents!'

'No chance!' His eyes were unreadable as he
helped her into his car. 'Maybe I'll explore your
personality. . .' Kate couldn't help resenting the fact
that his eyes were firmly fixed on what had once been
referred to as her greatest assets '. . .particularly
after a provocative remark like that!' he drawled.
'Let's go!'

'You've got a nerve!' she answered scornfully, but
his only reply was a twist of his lips. It's a good thing
I'm not scared of speed! Kate told herself as the
Porsche leapt forward as if pleased to be released
from this rather unfashionable and cheap part of
London which was the only place she could afford to
live in a small flat by herself.

Walking into a room with Ace next to her was
something of a revelation. Trying not to blink under
the hail of camera flashes, she felt an immediate and
unwanted affinity with royalty. Imagine having to go
through with this whenever one went out! Still she
lifted her chin slightly and tried to ignore the media
attention, knowing that it was all really centred on
Ace and that she was nothing more than a decorative
addition to his charismatic presence.

After a bit she became used to being stared at,
even taking it as a compliment. She supposed it was
all right when one was all dressed up, but perhaps it
could become a nightmare if one totally lost one's
privacy to move around anonymously.

'You're new, aren't you?' One of the Pressmen was doing his own bit of asset-stripping as his eyes roved intimately over her body. 'I haven't seen you around with Ace before. Where did he pick you up?'

Furious at being treated as if she were a brainless bimbo, she raised her eyebrows, giving him back such a measured look that he actually coloured a little and moved away.

'I don't think that's any of your business, is it? But, just for your *information*——' she underlined the last word '—I've known Ace Barton for more than ten years. . .'

'You must have been a kid in school! I didn't know he went for them that young!' The journalist had recovered and was fighting back.

'He was a friend of my family,' she finished, her tone dismissive. A speculative look was in her tormentor's eyes but before he could start working on her she was rescued.

'Come on, sweetie, don't waste any more time trading insults with this scumbag here!' Ace's eyes were full of mocking laughter as they took in the discomfited expression on the journalist's face. 'He's just trying to provoke you into giving an indiscreet answer that he can misquote. . .'

He pulled her away, and although there was a laughing expression on his face his voice was quiet as he continued to warn her about the power of the Press and how it was politic not to get up their nose whatever the provocation offered.

'Now come and meet the chief sponsor. He didn't believe me when I told him about you, which just goes to show how much people judge by outward appearances. He thought you had to be a model or a dancer, or else something in showbiz. He nearly had a coronary when I told him you were a fuel technician with IMP!' Kate's expression was hardly conciliatory, and he had to remind her in a fierce whisper that he was an important sponsor, so that she allowed herself to smile and be polite.

Ace took her on to a small but discreet restaurant where the food was delicious, but she found she didn't have much appetite. Too much excitement, she warned herself, because of course that was what it was. Ace's proximity was playing hell with her hormones. She'd always heard that his charm was legendary as far as women were concerned and this evening was certainly proving the truth of it.

Extraordinarily enough for a couple who were supposed to be at such odds, they seem to have no problem over their conversation. Ace filled in gaps for her as they talked about his long climb up to Formula One and his present position, and because of her background she was able to fill in the bare facts that he offered. It hadn't been an easy task, and in spite of his burning ambition and will to succeed. He loved driving and no doubt would always do so, but Kate discovered that there was a realist behind the glamorous image.

Over coffee she asked what she knew had to be the silliest question in the world.

'Are you afraid? I mean when you spun off last year and broke your ankle did you think that it might be, well, worse?' He looked away, the blue eyes somehow distant as if he was marshalling his thoughts.

'I take risks, but they're calculated risks and I wouldn't take them if I didn't think they had a good chance of succeeding. It's a pretty lonely business when you're out there on the track. You do your homework and hope that the rest of the team have done their best because it's your life that's out on the grid at the start. I suppose I believe in fate. If something's going to happen, it will happen, but in my case I take damned good care to check everything out first. To have an accident because one neglected to do one's job properly, well——' he shrugged his shoulders French-fashion '—in my book that would be unforgivable.'

He took a sip of his drink. 'Nowadays, as you found out this evening, it's big business that rules the sport. What the sponsor wants we try to see he gets, and that's why a great deal of my time is spent being seen where they want me to be seen, like tonight's cocktail party. So most of the time I'm an exile. It isn't forever, I know, but there are times when I wonder if I'm not missing out on other things that can be equally important.'

Kate was curious. 'What other things?'

'Like belonging and having proper homes instead of anonymous apartments in Monaco and London!' There was a ring of sadness in his voice which she found puzzling until she remembered something from the past—Eddie's voice repeating what he'd told her all those years ago at the Oulton Park circuit. 'Ace's a lucky devil. He hasn't got any family to worry him. . .' Kate remembered those words, and the undertone of bitterness in her brother's voice which she'd found incomprehensible at the time.

'I shouldn't think there have been any shortage of women in your life who would have been delighted to make a home for you anywhere in the world!' she told him waspishly, disliking the way he was making her feel a little sorry for him. Sorry indeed! World champion, and well on the way to winning it for a second time. What more did the man want? That 'little grey home in the west' idea wasn't going to fool her for a minute; it was easy to see that the man sitting next to her loved every minute of his fast-living, action-packed life.

A surprisingly warm smile made her turn and frown at him.

'You're not going to believe half the things I tell you, are you?'

She hunched her shoulders a little. 'Well, no, not when I know perfectly well that you love every minute of your life!' she challenged.

'Not quite every minute, but on balance, yes, I suppose I'm pretty happy with my job. At least you know that's true, that it is just a job, not the glamorous lifestyle that it appears to be, entailing flying around the world in private jets. I spend hours of time with my engineers, briefing, de-briefing, briefing again. I never know why the wives and girlfriends put up with it. . .'

Kate leant her chin on her hands as she considered his last words. Eventually she answered. 'I know so much about it, from a working point of view, that is, that I can't really envisage how it would feel to be such a complete outsider, and yet privately so necessary to someone. I suppose it could be because they feel part of such a tiny élite. I mean, there are only about thirty of you in Formula One, and there's no denying that the Press turn you into sort of demigods. . .'

Ace's eyes were acute as they studied her expression. 'You're refreshing to be with, Kate. That logical mind of yours isn't going to stand any nonsense, is it? In your eyes we're just rather ordinary men with quick reactions——'

'Hardly that!' she interrupted. 'Of course you've all got special personalities. You do dangerous things and take them in your stride just for starters. You have to keep yourselves very fit as well, and no doubt you have king-sized egos, which is why the motivation lasts. You all love every minute of the attention you get!'

There was no denying that she'd caught his interest. 'So it's rather what I thought. You're not dazzled by our charms.'

She tried hard not to consider the man sitting next to her and to answer the question logically. 'That's rather difficult, isn't it? I mean you're unusually tall for a driver, but most of them have to be fairly short. Also you have to be so narrowly motivated and self-contained if you're going to succeed. . . I mean most of the drivers I've seen aren't that attractive!' Ace gave an exaggerated wince. 'I read somewhere, and I think it's true, that it's your overalls that give that surface sex appeal,' she finished triumphantly.

'In other words Nomex is our aphrodisiac!' her companion laughed back at her.

Kate shrugged her shoulders. 'Why not? Uniforms have always been attractive to certain women, and the flame-retardant overalls have become pretty much a uniform.

'You almost convince me to go home and change!' he teased softly. 'You've certainly managed to cut my ego back down to size. Shall we go on and dance somewhere?'

'Why not?' she agreed lightly, hoping he wouldn't notice that his question had thrown her off balance. 'But I have to warn you in advance that I'm not a very good dancer. I haven't had enough practice.'

'Don't run yourself down, Kate. You move very gracefully, so I imagine you dance beautifully, and it has to be entirely your own fault you're not out dancing every night of your life!' His voice sounded so matter-of-fact that she had little difficulty in ignoring the more flattering words.

She gave him a quick look out of the corner of her eyes. 'Maybe,' she acknowledged, 'but I do work quite hard, and often for long hours, which means I'm often too tired to go out.'

He raised a quizzical eyebrow. 'If you want to be with someone, then tiredness doesn't come into it.'

'I suppose. . . Anyway I'm not naïve enough to forget that if we go dancing you'll immediately be surrounded by hundreds of your female fans!' She gave him a scornful look. 'I suppose that's why you want to go on—you're missing your usual dose of female adulation!'

One eyebrow was raised. 'Not that I have any wish to flatter you, but I have to admit that your some-times acerbic comments have come as a welcome change. If the fans are around it'll be your job this evening to keep them away!' he argued, his eyes dancing with amusement as he took in her affronted expression.

'I'll have to be sure of your total co-operation,' she countered sweetly, trying to deny the treacherous spread of warmth at the thought of dancing with him.

'You'll have it, Kate. Scout's honour!' Once more the blue eyes moved over her body with appreci-ation, confusing yet exciting her at the same time. She wished she weren't so naïve as far as men were concerned. Ace had been giving her conflicting mess-ages ever since the first time they'd met again outside her bedroom door in France. At the time she'd put that pass down to a reflex action of a man who couldn't let any opportunity pass him by, but now she was beginning to have doubts that he was as shallow as she'd first thought.

She'd spent the whole evening trying half-heart-edly to fight the inevitable attraction she felt for him. She even had reservations about his admitted feelings about her — at least if he went on looking at her like that.

She had to admit later, on renewing her lipstick in the Ladies', that it was fun being seen out with such a charismatic man. Everyone noticed him and either wanted to have a word or an acknowledgement of their recognition. It was Kate's first real outing with a celebrity, and she was finding it fun, particularly as he was gratifyingly attentive to her, even if it was out of self-interest.

Of course there was the occasional hiccup, such as when they'd arrived at the nightclub to see a particularly gorgeous girl whom the Press had linked with Ace in the past. Kate had been all too aware of the stiffening in the figure next to her, even if he had ignored the girl, apart from an acknowledging, casual smile in her direction.

It was a nasty shock therefore to be stopped by yet another dramatically good-looking girl in a vivid scarlet dress whom she'd noticed earlier ignoring her companion, her whole attention focused on Ace.

Dark red fingernails pressed uncomfortably into the flesh of her arm. 'Why, darling, I don't think we've met, have we?' The hint of a foreign accent on the uncomfortably accented word 'darling' warned Kate that this could be trouble.

She raised her own brows in slightly disdainful surprise, trying to make it clear she wasn't at all interested in getting to know this beautiful stranger.

'No, we haven't. Excuse me. . .' She removed the girl's hand from her arm rather ostentatiously before making for the door, but she wasn't allowed to get away with it.

'So?' Rather like a beautiful animal, the other woman seemed to have sensed Kate's own confusion and mixed-up feelings, because she at once took charge. 'We must join up then for the rest of the evening, yes? Then the evening will not be quite wasted for Ace. . . He is so seldom able to stay in London.'

'Join up? Why should we?'

The girl gave her a pitying smile. 'I'm Dara. . .'
Seeing this had no effect, she continued, 'Ace cut
our date last night because of you!'

Kate was quite unable to offer any more resist-
ance, in fact was so busy mentally castigating herself
for the happy daydreams she had had while dancing
with Ace that Dara had little need of her determination to take control of the rest of the evening.

With Dara once more clinging firmly and rather
painfully to her arm she was walked back to the
small, intimate table they had been sharing on the
edge of the small dance-floor, but Ace was quickly
on to his feet, side-stepping Dara's attempt to greet
him with a kiss.

Kate, freed at last, was discreetly rubbing her arm,
to find it firmly gripped again, but this time by Ace.

'Dara, great to see you! Sorry about last night! Do
you two girls know each other?'

Kate, on the receiving end of a warning nip, spoke
up. 'No, we met just now. . .'

'What a shame we can't stay. Mickey's invited us
to a party at his house, and no one turns down an
invite to Mickey's! Collect your coat, Kate. I'll meet
you at the bar.'

Realising she'd been dismissed, Kate did as she
was bidden, but there was a thoughtful look on her
face as she took in Dara's furious expression and
Ace's non-committal one.

So Ace had been teaching Dara a lesson, had he?
And she was being used to rub the message home.
Oh, well — she shrugged her shoulders — it would be

as well to remember the sort of girls he was used to being seen around with. For all her university degrees Kate was in the kindergarten class when it came to managing and understanding men, and she'd do well to remember it. Dara had handled her with humiliating ease, and no doubt could continue to do so if their paths were ever to cross again.

She'd no idea why Ace should have broken his date with Dara to spend the evening with her, but it certainly looked as if by doing so he'd stirred up some pretty powerful emotions. Kate wasn't particularly fanciful, but Dara reminded her of a black panther she'd seen once in a zoo. That, too, had been expressing its displeasure with rhythmic twitching of its powerful tail, its burning eyes fixed balefully on the visitors walking in front of its enclosure. She wondered if she'd walk out into a scene, or whether Ace had managed to extricate himself unscathed from the encounter as she left the relative comfort of the ladies' room.

He was waiting for her outside and wasted little time in virtually hustling her outside to where his car was waiting for them.

'Sorry about that, Kate. I hope you understand?' He tipped the commissionaire, then slid in to sit beside her. 'Dara's got all the charm of a queen wasp at the moment. She seems to think that, just because she fancies me the feeling should be mutual!'

Kate immediately began to feel sorry for Dara. 'I should think she has good reason to think like that,' she told him. 'She's a very beautiful woman.'

'Come on, she doesn't need you to blow her trumpet.'

Kate wasn't at all sure she liked hearing the cynical cruelty in his voice.

'People can't always control their feelings!' she answered coldly.

'That sort can! And I'm not in the habit of taking advantage of girls who don't know any better.'

'You might make a mistake one day,' she told him, her voice still cold. 'Not all beautiful women are as hard as you make out!'

'The ones that hang around the racetracks of the world are!' he responded. 'It's an education to see how they lie and cheat their way into getting passes for the paddock!'

Kate hunched a pettish shoulder. 'Surely that doesn't apply to Dara?' She was trying hard to deny to herself that *she* had any feelings for him.

He gave a reluctant laugh. 'No, of course not; her tactics are slightly more subtle, although you never know. . .' He remained silent, obviously thinking hard. 'I suppose it's not surprising you don't understand—you'd never behave like that, would never have any need to. . .When I stay in hotels around the world, do you know I get photos of naked women pushed under my door with phone numbers on them? It isn't pretty, the lengths some women will go to to sleep with one of the drivers.'

This had her feeling ashamed of her sex.

'No. . .' Ace's voice continued reflectively. 'You're very naïve, aren't you, for someone your age?'

'Am I?' she responded coldly.

'Are you involved with anyone — seriously I mean?'

She was surprised at the question, and debated whether to answer it truthfully or not, then, with a mental shrug, said, 'No, not really, not anyone important. . .'

'Will you help me out of jam, then?'

'Why, yes. . . No! Why should I?'

He heard the surprise in her voice, and smiled a little at having so nearly caught her out. 'Will you pretend to be my girlfriend for the next few months?'

Kate was completely flabbergasted. The silence lasted until the Porsche pulled up outside the converted house that contained her tiny flat.

'Well?' There was amusement in his voice. 'Don't keep me in suspense!'

'You're mad! I don't even like you; you're virtually blackmailing me to work for you, and now you want me to pretend to be your girlfriend?' They had both undone their seatbelts and had turned to face each other, the dim streetlighting giving their faces a ghostly orange pallor.

'I'm completely serious!' He looked down at his hands. 'You saw what happened tonight. I don't want that to happen again. Nor do I feel like setting myself up as an Aunt Sally just waiting for all those girls to throw themselves at me in the attempt to knock me off my perch!'

Kate tried hard but it was too much. She giggled; she couldn't help it. 'I wasn't much help this evening.' Now why had she said that?'

'She'll leave me alone once she sees I'm serious about you!'

Kate couldn't help a small shiver running down her back at his words, but he misinterpreted it. 'I'm sorry, Kate, you're cold! Can we finish this discussion in your flat?'

He had said 'pretend', hadn't he? she told herself as she nodded agreement.

'Would you like a coffee?' she asked, as she opened the door to her flat.

'Yes, please.'

'It's only instant; do you mind?'

'Not a bit.' He came into the kitchen with her, perching upon one of units and watching her as she boiled the kettle and took down a couple of mugs. When she'd finished and given it to him, they both sat at her tiny kitchen table.

'If you agree, Kate, it'll mean killing two birds with one stone.'

'What do you mean?'

'Once you start to work with me no one will believe we're not lovers. . .'

'Oh, yes, they will!' Her eyes had narrowed fiercely. 'They'll know because I shall take great pleasure in telling everyone the truth!'

'You're forgetting something!'

She looked back at him shocked. 'You wouldn't!'

'I most certainly would! You needn't get in a panic, I won't come near you, except in public. . .'

'Do you mean you want me to share. . .?' She wasn't able to finish, but Ace had no qualms.

'Certainly! They nearly always give me a suite, so you'll have your own room——'

'No! I won't do it!'

'Funny. Now why did I get the impression that you cared what happens to your father? He had to sell his business, didn't he, to pay off Eddie's debts?'

'You bastard!'

Ace shrugged his shoulders. 'Not as far as I know, but you're taking a pretty selfish attitude over this, aren't you? Your dear brother left quite a few problems behind when he failed to take that corner. Perhaps you don't think your family have already suffered enough?'

'What about me? Why make me pay for what Eddie did?'

'Yes, that's your bad luck, isn't it? Maybe you would have been safer if you'd not chosen a career that could involve you with mine.'

If she accepted this crazy proposal of his then she'd be committing herself to a course of action that could be supremely dangerous to her. Would she be strong enough to resist his powerful sexuality if they were to spend virtually all their time together? On the other hand, did she have any choice?

'Why does it have to be me?' she protested. 'I'm no good at play-acting. Everyone will soon know the truth if they start asking me questions.'

'Nonsense, you're not thinking this out properly. You're quite capable of dealing out "no comment" to any of the Press brave enough to tackle you, and anyone else, I should have thought!'

'Why couldn't you have cast Dara in this role of

your girlfriend? She looks the part and no doubt would enjoy every minute of it.'

'That's why.'

'That's perverse!' she protested.

He shrugged. 'If you say so.' He appeared suddenly bored. 'Stop making such a meal of it, Kate. You and I know there's nothing to it, so why get uptight about a lot of Press comment?'

'Because it's my reputation!' she answered fiercely. 'I'm not one of your empty-headed bimbos grateful for any attention your ego can spare. I've built up my career in an area where women are not generally accepted, and just being seen as your girlfriend is going to lose me a lot of respect!'

Ace looked at her with astonishment. 'So you are a feminist after all!'

'No, I'm not.'

'So what's so terrible about being known as my girlfriend?' he asked, genuinely puzzled.

Kate looked at him with growing scorn. 'Come on, Ace, you can't be that thick! None of your so-called friends look as if they have exactly been renowned for their brains, do they?'

He grinned at her. 'You're an intellectual snob! It'll do you good to join the rest of the human race for a change. I don't think the rarefied air of the laboratory agrees with you! Anyway, you shouldn't judge by appearances. Why, you're as bad as old Sir Harry at the drinks this evening. . . He thought you were a ——'

'I know quite well what the old goat thought I

was,' Kate interrupted, 'and if anything that bears out my case!'

Ace stood up. 'I'm sorry, Kate. That's a cross you're going to have to bear. Thanks for the coffee; I'll be in touch. . .' He gave a faintly malicious smile at her furious expression and walked out of her flat.

CHAPTER FOUR

KATE went to work the next day rather ashamed of the absurdly flattering photo of herself which had made the gossip column of her daily paper. She tried hard not to appear self-conscious as she greeted the doorman at IMP's headquarters where she worked.

She was greeted with raillery from her fellow workers, but Jason surprisingly wasn't around. It wasn't easy to pretend to be casual under their teasing, but she hoped she managed to conceal her real feelings. Guessing what might greet her in the canteen, she opted for sandwiches in the laboratory, but because today no one else on the team was prepared to forgo his lunch-hour proper she was on her own until she was interrupted.

'Will you come into my office, Kate?' She looked up in surprise to see Jason with an unusually serious expression on his face. She wiped the crumbs off her fingers, and, taking a final gulp of her coffee, stood up and answered,

'Sure.'

He strode on ahead of her, rather than waiting for her to join him as he would normally have done, and the slightly calculated rudeness had her frowning as she followed him into his office.

Her surprise turned rapidly to wariness when she saw on his desk a number of daily papers, all with photographs of her and Ace in them. He sat down, and without waiting to be asked she too relaxed into the familiar chair in front of his desk.

Jason gestured with one hand. 'Perhaps you'd care to explain this to me.'

Kate was at first astounded by his arrogance, then furiously angry. 'Explain what? My private life? You've got a nerve, Jason.'

He sat forward and coloured faintly. 'I think I've a perfect right to ask, certainly when an employee's lifestyle is likely to affect the company,' he finished pompously.

'You've got to be joking! I've no intention of sharing my private life with you or anyone else who works with IMP.'

'You're a fool, Kate, but I must say I never thought you'd open up to someone like him. Why, in a few months it'll all be finished, and then you'll be left high and dry!'

'Why are you speaking to me like this? You've no right.' Kate had two bright spots of colour in her cheeks.

'As head of your team, I have every right if I think your behaviour is going to put our working relationship at risk.'

Kate couldn't help her look of blank astonishment. Jason was obviously suffering under some strong emotion. Where was the rational scientist she'd hoped she'd be working under this last year?

'I just don't believe what I'm hearing!' She shook her head, as if trying to clear it. 'I signed a contract when I came to work here. It had a number of clauses in it designed quite properly to protect the company, but there wasn't one, not one, that was relevant to my private life. If there had been I wouldn't have come here to work, and you know that fact quite well, so forget your so-called "rights",' she finished scornfully.

Jason looked down and fiddled with a pencil on his desk. 'Are you Ace Barton's latest girlfriend?' he enquired with a note in his voice she couldn't quite recognise.

'And if I am? What's so terrible for IMP in that?' she blustered, still bewildered why he should find the idea of it so important.

He had the grace to look a little ashamed, then stood up quickly, pushing his chair out of the way. 'I'm afraid it hasn't worked out having a woman on the team, Kate.' He risked a quick look at her furious face. 'Oh, I know your research has been successful, but you're too inclined to work on your own, not to share your thinking with your colleagues. I like to think of us all as a successful unit and it's disruptive for the others if one member persistently refuses to conform as you do.' He turned his back on her to look out of the window. 'In the circumstances, I think it would be better if you'd tender your resignation. . .'

Kate looked at his rigid, unyielding back with narrowed eyes. 'You mean it would be better for you if I left, don't you?' she demanded.

'I don't know what you're talking about. . .' he blustered, turning to face her, trying not to acknowledge what he saw written on her face. The scales had fallen from her eyes and she saw all too clearly what perhaps she should have been aware of earlier. Jason was jealous of her ability to come up with consistently good ideas and saw her as a threat to his career. He was going to take any opportunity he could to get her off his team, so there was little point in her trying to argue her case with him. All the same she didn't see why she should give in without a fight. She realised, with hindsight, that he hadn't forgiven her either for turning him down soon after she'd joined the team.

She was rescued when the door behind her suddenly opened and one of the junior chemists put his head round the door.

'Get out!' Jason ordered. 'Can't you see I'm busy?' But Kate took the opportunity to slip out past the young man, even though her boss yelled at her to stay.

'What on earth was that all about?' the young man queried, looking quite shaken as he hurriedly closed the door, but Kate, feeling quite unable to tell him anything, just grimaced and blindly walked away.

Lord, what a muddle! If anyone thought she'd go back to the laboratory and behave as if nothing had happened then they wanted their head examined. But as she walked quickly through the enormous building she began to have doubts. Jason had never done anything overtly wrong as far as she was concerned until his outburst today. She was feeling hurt and a little bewildered. Had he really only taken her on because he fancied her and thought she'd never be a threat to his position?

One thing was certain. If she walked back into the laboratory Jason would engineer a scene. She would certainly lose her job and might even be putting other of her colleagues at risk. A number of them were under few illusions as to the value of her work. She bit her lip in indecision before once more walking purposefully towards one of the lifts. This was a problem that merited expert advice, and, although she'd only met the personnel director once before, she'd liked him.

'Ah, yes.' Robert Dexter greeted her with a smile. 'The board were talking about you earlier this week. Our hidden asset, so to speak, if you'll forgive us.' A particularly charming smile ensured she'd not take offence at his words. 'We were wondering if perhaps you'd consider taking a more high-profile role in the company?'

Still shaken and bemused by what had happened, she looked back at him blankly.

'I see I'll have to explain. . .' He gave her a shrewd look. 'To put it bluntly, we wondered whether you'd consider taking a sabbatical for six months or so from your backroom job to liaise direct with Carlisle Flint? You seem to have impressed our number-one driver as well, because he too has asked if you could be released to work closely with him for the rest of the season. You'd be on the line for a certain amount of publicity, but I've been looking at today's papers and it seems you've already had a taste of what the Press can be like. . .' His eyes dropped discreetly to his desk and Kate noticed that his paper too had a picture of her with Ace. Her lips tightened a little at what he must be thinking, but it didn't take long for her to decide that here she had the perfect lead-in to her problem.

Kate told him what had just happened in Jason's office. He gave her a shrewd look. 'Do you want to pursue this matter?'

She shook her head. 'Jason has been my boss for the last year, and as far as I was concerned a reasonably good one. I don't know why he's suddenly decided he wants me off the team. . .' Diplomatically she accepted it would be better not to mention that it was jealousy about her ideas. 'But I feel it's a bit unfair that he should try to use a few Press photographs as an excuse!'

Robert Dexter's eyes were shrewd in understanding as he returned her look, but it seemed as if he too realised the wisdom of not putting thoughts into words.

'I had a meeting with him here this morning. He was quite eloquent in agreeing that it would be a good idea to see what you could accomplish on your own without his back up. . .' There was a small silence. 'On balance then it seems as if this change we have suggested might be a good thing. Unless of course you wish to leave the company?'

'No, not while there's still a job for me.' She had looked faintly horrified at his suggestion.

'That's what I hoped you'd say.' He smiled at her. 'Naturally we're hoping that you'll continue to use your skills on the front line, so to speak, but the advertising department are hoping to use you for a bit of company PR. Would you have any objections?'

Kate smiled, then shrugged her shoulders. 'Well, no, not really, but I don't know anything about PR work. All the same I don't suppose you'd keep me on my salary unless I was working most of the time, would you? I mean if I'm not working in the lab then there are going to be times when I shall be short of a job. . .' Her anxious query was not lost on the man sitting opposite her.

'As the suggestion to temporarily change your job has come from us I think you'll find that the company will be generous. As to that other matter——' he stood up and came round his desk '—I don't have to ask you to be discreet, do I? It would be a pity if this story got about, don't you agree?'

Kate's colour rose higher. 'You needn't be worried anyone will hear anything from me, but we were interrupted by one of the junior chemists.'

'I'll take care of that,' he said briskly, 'and I know everyone will be more than grateful to you for your understanding over this—er—matter.' He held out a hand to her. 'Shall I get someone to clear your things? I imagine you'd prefer not to put your head back— er—in the lion's den just at the moment!'

Kate gave him a grateful smile. 'This idea of a job change has come with perfect timing, hasn't it? Anyway there's been nothing to regret as far as I'm concerned. When am I supposed to liaise with Carlisle Flint?'

'I don't think Mike Booker is expecting you until the team leaves for Estoril, so you'll have three or four days to find your feet. Good luck!' He stood up and shook her hand.

Kate left his office wondering about the hand of fate. Ace had spoken of his intention to try and pull strings on her behalf, but she hadn't thought he'd have that much clout with a multi-national the size of IMP. She wondered what the advertising people had in mind for her and hoped it wouldn't be anything too drastic. In fact on balance she thought it might be very interesting to be on the spot when the cars were tested for real instead of waiting in the laboratory for the print-outs and reports from whichever of the team was out there. She supposed she'd take over that duty, which possibly would make her unpopular back in the lab. Oh, well, there was no point in speculating about what might be. . . She left the building in a dream, serenely unaware that her so-called relationship with Ace was the hottest piece of gossip from the boardroom downwards.

She got back to her flat to find the phone ringing. 'Yes?' she answered, her voice guarded in case it was Jason who was calling. She felt bad about leaving without saying goodbye, but what else was she supposed to do?

'Hi! You look great in the pix. . .'

'Oh, Ace, it's you!'

'You sound relieved. What's been happening at IMP? I tried to call you there but was told you'd left for home.'

'It's a little more complicated than that,' she told him, annoyed that she'd betrayed herself, 'but you needn't try to exert your influence on the company. They'd apparently already decided to loan me to Carlisle Flint. Talk about fate!'

'They had?' He sounded amused. 'I can't say I'm surprised. So they've decided to exploit your beauty and your brains, have they?'

'I'm told they might need me for a bit of PR work, but basically I gather I'm going to be the technician permanently with the team.'

'I don't suppose that's made you many friends back in the lab. Those boys used to enjoy their stint on the tracks with us.'

'I don't think my being there will change it too much. They'll probably still send somebody, but perhaps only one rather than two.' Her voice was dismissive, almost offhand. She hoped that Jason would keep his mouth shut about his doubts over her work.

'So no problems about you leaving?' he queried.

'None!' she replied quickly—perhaps too quickly?

'I see that whatever they were you're not prepared to share them with anyone.' Was that a note of pique in his voice? She decided that perhaps honesty was going to be the best policy after all.

'Well, there was a little problem, but I don't think I'd better talk about it on the phone.' Once again her voice sounded dismissive to the listening man.

'What are your immediate plans, then?' Ace demanded.

'I haven't dared make any!' she responded sarcastically. 'I thought that was your department now?'

'It makes my plans a great deal easier anyway.' It seemed he was going to ignore her bitter little comment. 'The *Citation* is standing by to pick us up. I thought we'd spend the next few days in Monaco, getting to know each other!' he finished outrageously.

Kate was in a quandary. On the one hand there was nothing she wanted to do more, but on the other, well, she objected strongly to being at his beck and call.

'Come on, Kate, don't be an idiot.' His voice was delightfully persuasive. 'OK, you'll be staying in my apartment there, but surely you know you'll be quite safe with me?'

That was indeed something that she knew all too well, but she wasn't particularly flattered to have it spelt out to her quite so categorically. Half of her didn't want to be safe with him, and he was obviously quite aware of that fact.

'I don't think I can be ready to leave this evening,' she answered primly. 'Perhaps tomorrow?'

'No way, Kate! I'm leaving this evening and you're coming with me, even if I have to help you pack, but don't bother with anything except the basics. You and I are going shopping at the other end.'

All the same it was Dr Kate Ash who was waiting for him in her small flat, dressed in one of her smart business suits, two matching cases ready by her side. Ace's mouth quirked in polite amusement, but he said nothing as she raised her chin in challenge.

'Ready?' He took hold of her luggage, and at her nod said, 'Let's go!'

Kate, having been prepared for a fight over the amount of her luggage, was left with the wind taken out of her sails. Dressed with extreme casualness himself in trainers and jeans, he ignored her outfit and she was left feeling uncomfortably in the wrong, almost as if he was doing her a favour by not commenting on her appearance.

It wasn't as though she'd expected him to wear a City suit. She knew perfectly well from the many Press photos of him that he preferred casual wear. It was just that she was making a statement herself in dressing up. It was her unspoken answer to his earlier bullying tactics on the phone.

She was painfully aware that if she ever betrayed her ambivalent feelings for him he would end their charade immediately with little or no compunction. By trying to concentrate on what she thought of as the negative parts of his personality she would protect her own weakness. Also it was about time he learnt that bossing her around wouldn't be a pushover for him.

She tried hard not to be too impressed with his private jet, although its luxury brought home to her just how great were the rewards of succeeding in Formula One. Ace watched her with his amusement ill-hidden, which she was beginning to find irritating. What was so funny about her? Still her pride refused to let her ask him why he found her company so amusing. She sank back into her extremely comfortable seat and, as Ace picked up a magazine to read, undid her attaché case and took out, it had to be admitted with some deliberate ostentation, notes on high-tech fuel consumption.

Her eyes flashed a fiery retort as she found the notes taken from her hand, and a magazine put there instead. 'Read this, Kate. You'll need to get your eye in before we go shopping tomorrow.' But she found she wasn't proof against his sudden closeness, nor his smiling charm as his eyes tried yet again to seek out the curves of her body hidden so discreetly from his probing by her chosen armour. She retired behind the glowing silken curtain of her loose hair as the jet began to taxi away from the small private terminal at London's second airport, her feelings in a turmoil.

Was she mad to have agreed to play this role in his life? Should she have called his bluff? She turned the pages of the fashion magazine over, but her eyes didn't take in any of the models so enticingly displayed in its pages; her attention was all focused inwards on herself.

'Regretting your decision already?' Ace demanded, freeing himself from the constraints of his seatbelt as the jet, now airborne, levelled off, and smiling at the stewardess who was bending over him with familiarity, offering what was obviously his normal choice of drink. He smiled his thanks, allowing his eyes to meet the girl's, and Kate found herself uncurling fingers that had suddenly dug nails into her palms.

When the girl approached her, Ace said, 'Try my special, Kate. I think you'll like it.' The girl was bending forward to serve her and Kate found herself meeting somewhat empty blue eyes surrounded by lashes that looked unnaturally heavy under the weight of too much black mascara. She felt a little ashamed of herself as the close-up revealed a skin no longer young under the false bloom of youth.

'Hi! Thanks, I will.' She smiled at the stewardess with real friendliness but she needn't have bothered because the answering smile was strictly professional. She's wasting no time on me, Kate thought, as she was deftly served before the girl turned back to show Ace her white teeth once again.

Kate took a sip, but refused to make any comment. 'I'd hardly call it my decision to be here with you. It seems to me all the decisions have been yours!'

'Good, I'm glad you're beginning to appreciate that fact!' He grinned at her. 'Seen anything you like?' He got up and came to squat next to her, flipping through the pages rather impatiently until he stopped suddenly. 'I rather thought that was pretty sensational. You've got the height to get away with it. . .'

Kate's eyes widened at the picture displayed. 'You don't honestly think I'd ever wear anything like that!' She risked a look at his expression and saw he was entirely serious.

'Why not?' I think you'd look terrific. There's nothing wrong with your legs, so what's so wrong in showing them off?'

Kate looked back at him, her expression perplexed. How was she to explain that she didn't go in for this high-profile look?

'You looked pretty good last night, Kate, but today, well, you look like some middle-aged housewife!' She sat up straight, her eyes once more flashing fire. 'Keep your cool, girl. Look, I know you're clever and you've made a success of a career in a male-dominated area, but there's no need to ram that fact down everyone's throat.'

His eyes were a warm clear blue as they fixed and held her dark ones. 'You're really ambivalent about what I've let you in for, aren't you?' Hypnotised, she just nodded.

'Look, Kate, I want you to relax and learn to have a bit of fun. You've been trying to over-compensate for Eddie's death for far too long.'

Her eyes widened in shock. How could he have guessed that had been her driving force?

'Don't look so horrified! There's nothing that drastically bad in behaving that way, but you've let it become a habit, one that you can't break out of very easily. Its about time you put the clock back, so to speak, and started to enjoy life again without feeling any guilt.'

She sat up in a kind of horror, her feelings filling her up with shame. 'Hey, what are you?' she demanded shakily. 'Some kind of amateur psychologist?'

'No, but maybe I could be a friend if you'd let me.' His eyes were neutral as they took in her shattered expression. 'First of all why don't you start by telling me just exactly what it was that upset you today?'

Caught off balance, Kate tried to keep her teetering emotions on an even keel as she strove to find the right words to explain what had happened in Jason's office.

'Jason Prior was livid when he read about our going out together last night. He asked me to resign, but I think that was just an excuse to get rid of me because he's jealous of my work!' she finished baldly, quite unable to dress up the truth.

'I was afraid something like this might happen to you.' He looked at her uncomprehending face. 'You haven't got the first idea of your impact on my sex, have you?' he demanded. 'I suppose you also turned down the chance to be his girlfriend?'

She gave him a resentful look. 'Of course I know some men find me attractive!' she snapped. 'I'd be an idiot if I didn't, but no one's ever wanted me to leave my job because of it!'

He shook his head at her. 'A girl with your sort of looks is sufficiently unusual in herself. Add brains to that particular package, and you're dynamite to someone like Jason Prior. Of course he can't forgive you! He knows you're better at his job and you turned him down flat. No wonder he's been looking for an excuse to get rid of you.'

He stood up. 'Don't look so stricken. He'll soon get over the damage you've done to his ego!'

Kate looked back at him curiously. He'd certainly spoken of her appeal with convincing sincerity. Quite without thinking, she spoke exactly what was in her mind.

'And you? Do you find me so special?' she couldn't help asking.

His face shuttered immediately, hiding all expression, making her wish she'd bitten her tongue out before allowing it to betray her so drastically.

'I've already told you that you don't need to worry about me, Kate. I might play games in public, but once we're alone together you can treat me as you would have done if Eddie were still alive.'

Kate found Ace's apartment beautiful but also fairly soulless. There seemed no real stamp of his personality anywhere, and it was very nearly as impersonal as a hotel room. His flat in London had more personality than this place. It didn't take her long to realise that he couldn't really be spending much time here.

Their relationship, though, was anything but bland. They started to disagree over the clothes Ace insisted on buying her until she was almost overcome with embarrassment. She knew he was rich but this was ridiculous. Anyway, accepting presents from him made her feel uncomfortable.

'Look!' she snapped after being dragged into yet another smart boutique. 'I've got enough clothes to last me a lifetime. I don't need any more.'

'You're going to be following the sun, sweetheart, and be honest and admit you haven't got a clue of what you'll need,' he teased.

'I'm not your sweetheart and I'll admit nothing of the kind!' she snapped back, unable to take any more. 'When you bullied me into this. . .charade,' she spat the words out, 'it didn't give you the right to boss me about. If I say I have enough clothes, I have enough clothes,' she finished.

Her crush on this man was beginning to wear very thin indeed after being in his company all day. Her pride had taken a hell of a beating at his hands because he was treating her exactly as if she were a sometimes tiresome younger sister. Not for one minute did his guard slip until she was forced to accept that that was exactly how he felt about her.

She in her turn had discovered a man who might be charismatic in public, but privately was one who was also ruthless, single-minded, and a loner, an attitude that disconcerted her, because she recognised similar traits in herself. Physically she had to admit he still turned her on and probably always would, but, having found out just how irritating he could be to live with she was furious to discover that his sex appeal was far too potent a force for her feelings to be seriously affected, no matter how cross with him she felt at the moment.

Ace pretended to look suddenly crushed by her fierce words, but she wasn't going to be fooled.

'Will you please stop laughing at me,' she told him fiercely, 'or at least have the decency to share the joke?'

'Laughing?' He spread his arms wide in negation. 'I don't laugh ——'

'Don't split hairs!' she interrupted. 'You do laugh, secretly.'

His eyes crinkled up in real amusement once more. 'Kate. . .' He took in the rising storm signals and tried to make himself look serious. 'Try not to let yourself get so intense about everything. You amuse me because you take yourself so seriously. . .' He risked a quick glance at her outraged expression. 'Don't you know when I'm teasing you?' he demanded, one eyebrow raised in query.

Kate took a deep breath. 'I don't like being

laughed at,' she told him, her face still stiff with offended pride. 'Anyway, I don't want you to tease me!' It was all very well, but she still didn't really understand why he found her so funny.

This time he couldn't help himself and he laughed outright, but he put his arm around her as he did so. 'Try not to be so touchy, and don't be a spoilsport. I think you'll look terrific in those hotpants, so let me buy them for you?'

Kate removed herself from the too close proximity. 'No, Ace. You're going to be working hard, and so am I. There'll be no time to wear anything like that; anyway, I don't like them!' She flounced out of the little shop, hoping he'd follow her. He kept her waiting a couple of minutes, which raised her suspicions, but when he walked out empty-handed she smiled inwardly at having won at least one small battle between them.

All the same she was mortified to discover on returning much later to the apartment that the detested clothes were waiting for her in her room. She had a severe struggle with herself, but decided that if she made a fuss she'd just make him laugh even more at her. The dignified thing would be to ignore them. After all, he might be able to buy them but he could hardly force her to wear them, could he? She already had grave doubts about the propriety of letting him buy her things, but accepted that it was part of the deal of being his supposed girlfriend.

When they weren't arguing they got on quite well talking about their careers. Ace in particular seemed genuinely interested in her work and, although she'd never really been fooled into thinking his life was a hedonistic round of pleasure apart from risking his life sixteen weekends a year, she was quite surprised at the dedication he displayed in keeping fit and the work he put in behind the scenes.

He had invested his money in a number of schemes that required his attention, and his days seemed pretty full to her untrained eyes. She came to realise that any woman who aimed to share his life would always have to be self-sufficient and able to cope with the day-to-day problems of life without bothering him with the minutiae of domestic detail.

She joined in the training sessions, but soon found to her chagrin that in the personal fitness stakes he left her standing. Ace, aware of her sense of inadequacy, asked Joe, his coach, to work out a programme specially for her. Once the trainer explained how it took time to bring the body up to peak fitness, she stopped trying to keep up and felt better for it.

They had four days together before they had to leave for Estoril and the pre-race qualifying sessions, and by the end of them Kate had to admit that the naïve dreams she'd had of becoming irresistible to this man were exactly that, and extremely unrealistic into the bargain.

Her own feelings swung so violently between attraction and a very real fear and hate of what he'd forced her to do that she was still as prickly as a porcupine in his presence, unless they were talking about work. She felt she had learned nothing about him as a man, that in some secret way he was keeping her at a distance.

Although this inspired her to try to find other areas
apart from work where they could communicate, he
seemed intent on repelling her curiosity, deftly turning her queries aside until she was forced to admit to
herself that he was as clever in his way as she was,
academically, in hers.

By mutual consent they hadn't eaten out, Ace
arranging for meals to be sent up to the apartment
from the Italian restaurant next door. Kate learnt
that pasta played an important part in his diet.

On their way to Estoril in the private jet Kate was
forced to admit to herself that he had won the first
round. He had treated her exactly as he'd said he
would, and not even for an instant had Kate had
even a bat's twinkling that he thought of her as an
attractive woman. He'd laughed at her, teased her,
and succeeded in keeping her at a distance.

Silently she brooded on her own thoughts, unwilling to admit to herself that he presented a challenge.
She had a lot to learn about the man inside Ace
Barton, world champion, and he was as different
from her original crush as anyone with a modicum of
brains should have expected. What had she really
known about the young man who'd been Eddie's
friend? Very little apart from his outward appearance, and when he hadn't been teasing her he'd been
carelessly kind to her when they met. The last time
they had met at Oulton Park he had unthinkingly
humiliated her, wounding her immature feelings, and
the pain had been intense. All the same, now she
was older she had to admit that what he'd done

wasn't so very terrible; she'd just reacted in an over-sensitive manner.

It was depressing to have to admit to herself that after four days together she was none the wiser, that, if she made the mistake again of leaving her vulnerable heart unguarded, he might once more strike her a casually cruel blow, and this time she might not recover. With a ruthlessness that would have been complimented by Ace if he'd known, she threw her mind totally back into her work.

'Ace?'

'Umm?' With reluctance he looked up from papers he was studying.

'Tell me about Estoril. The track, I mean.'

He allowed his papers to drop on to the cabin floor, and his eyes lit up with interest.

'I think it's a driver's track. It's bumpy, and demanding, but you get a good race on it. It's a combination of high- and medium-speed corners, which means you really have to concentrate on your handling, and you need plenty of aerodynamic downforce. Brakes and tyres both take a battering, and the chassis set-up is vital. . .' He talked on, giving her a driver's run-down, and she narrowed her attention span to concentrate exactly on his words.

When they met up with the rest of the Carlisle Flint team Kate tried to ignore the studiously impassive face of Mike Booker as he greeted her. She couldn't help but wonder what he was thinking, and allowed herself a sour internal smile at the thought that only she and Ace knew he had to be wrong. Being his girlfriend wasn't exactly going to do her image with the rest of the team much good either. It would be all too easy for them to forget her professionalism down at Paul Ricard.

Not surprisingly Ace had little time for her except for her job as fuel technician as the run-up to the race started, but Kate had forgotten the media. Her few days in Monaco, relatively untroubled by the Press, not even the paparazzi bothering her, were at an end.

Her relationship with Ace was news. She was news. Everyone in Carlisle Flint wanted a run-down on her personal affairs. Suddenly it seemed to her as if the whole world wanted to know about every detail of her life. Her only escape was in the paddock, in the motor home or the pits, where she scowled ferociously if disturbed from her work, and even there the journalists sometimes prowled, always on the look-out for a good story.

Mindful of Ace's warning, she kept her cool, but it wasn't easy, and the final straw was when Jason himself turned up as chief fuel technician. She had only to take one look at him to realise he hadn't forgiven her for walking out on him, nor for going to see Robert Dexter behind his back, and her heart sank. She didn't think it was going to take long before he somehow caused trouble for her.

Ace was out on the track, testing. There was nothing she could do to warn him about trouble except beat a hasty retreat back to their hotel suite in Cascais before Jason could catch up with her. If she walked out, then he would be unable to follow

NO COST! NO OBLIGATION TO BUY! NO PURCHASE NECESSARY!

PLAY "LUCKY 7"
AND GET AS MANY AS SIX FREE GIFTS...

HOW TO PLAY:

1 With a coin, carefully scratch off the silver box opposite. You will now be eligible to receive two or more FREE books, and possibly other gifts, depending on what is revealed beneath the scratch off area.

2 When you return this card, you'll receive specially selected Mills & Boon Romances. We'll send you the books and gifts you qualify for absolutely FREE, and at the same time we'll reserve you a subscription to our Reader Service.

3 If we don't hear from you within 10 days, we'll then send you four brand new Romances to read and enjoy every month for just £1.80 each, the same price as the books in the shops. There is no extra charge for postage and handling. There are no hidden extras.

4 When you join the Mills & Boon Reader Service, you'll also get our free monthly Newsletter, featuring author news, horoscopes, penfriends and competitions.

5 You are under no obligation, and may cancel or suspend your subscription at any time simply by writing to us.

You'll love your cuddly teddy. His brown eyes and cute face are sure to make you smile.

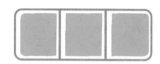

Play "Lucky 7"

Just scratch off the silver box with a coin.
Then check below to see which gifts you get.

YES! I have scratched off the silver box. Please send me all the gifts for which I qualify. I understand that I am under no obligation to purchase any books, as explained on the opposite page. I am over 18 years of age.

MS/MRS/MISS/MR _____ 6A3R

ADDRESS _____

_____

POSTCODE _____ SIGNATURE _____

7 7 7	**WORTH FOUR FREE BOOKS** FREE TEDDY BEAR AND MYSTERY GIFT
🔔🔔🔔	**WORTH FOUR FREE BOOKS** AND MYSTERY GIFT
🍒🍒🍒	**WORTH FOUR FREE BOOKS**
🍒🔔 BAR	**WORTH TWO FREE BOOKS**

MILLS & BOON "NO RISK" GUARANTEE

* You're not required to buy a single book!
* You must be completely satisfied or you may cancel at any time simply by writing to us. You will receive no more books; you'll have no further obligation.
* The free books and gifts you receive from this offer remain yours to keep no matter what you decide.

If offer details are missing, write to:
Mills & Boon Reader Service, P.O. Box 236, Croydon, Surrey CR9 9EL

Mills & Boon Reader Service
FREEPOST
P.O. Box 236
Croydon
Surrey
CR9 9EL

NO
STAMP
NEEDED

her unless he'd brought back-up with him, and somehow she rather doubted that he had.

He'd come out here to try to make trouble over her work, but luckily everything was going so well that he'd find that difficult. One thing she'd learned from Ace in the short time they'd been together was to be quick on her feet. She didn't feel she could bother Mike with the problem either; he might be team manager, but like everyone else his thoughts were closely tied up in the cars and their drivers. She left the track without a backward look, intent on hiding in the hotel suite until Ace returned to rescue her.

Two hours later Ace walked in with an expression on his face that had her standing up, her face turning scarlet with mortification.

'W-what's happened?' she stuttered, suddenly and quite unaccountably nervous.

'That new fuel blend of yours has just ensured that I've had the most embarrassing drive of my life! The car faded every time I lifted my foot. I was a fool to trust you, wasn't I?' he snarled.

'What? Don't be silly, Ace. There was nothing wrong with either drive yesterday. It can't be the fuel.'

'Really? Well, you'd better be prepared to take that up with Mike and the boys. Thank God your ex-boss has turned up. He's down there now working flat out to correct your almighty cock-up!'

Kate's heart sank. 'I'd better get down there myself. . .'

'I shouldn't bother, sweetheart! I don't think the

boys are too keen to have you around at the moment, and I can't say I blame them. I might have guessed you'd something worked out in the way of revenge, but your timing's gone a bit wrong. I bet this wasn't planned to happen until we were racing, was it?'

Kate looked at him, every vestige of colour having left her face.

'No! There was nothing wrong with my fuel blend. It has to be something else. I'm going to find out for myself.' A strong arm barred her from leaving the room.

'Oh, no! You aren't going anywhere where there's the slightest chance that you could cause more trouble. I want your pass back, Kate; I promised Mike.'

CHAPTER FIVE

KATE was left sitting alone once more as Ace stormed off, but she hardly noticed he'd gone because all she could think about was how the fuel blend had let them down. Her logical brain checked and checked again, but she knew that the problems described to her by Ace couldn't be her fault. Suddenly unable to sit still, she stood up and began pacing the floor until she ended up sitting by the phone. IMP had to have the latest print-outs of the disaster.

Half an hour later she was sitting cross-legged on the floor trying to come to terms with the lengths Jason Prior had gone to to blacken her reputation and safeguard his job. Luckily she had proof, because she didn't think it was going to take long before he took steps to make it seem as if she'd made a criminally stupid error. Paul had been one of her chums on the team, and she knew she could depend on him to get her work independently analysed by another department — at least she hoped she could, because he seemed to think Jason had simply made a mistake. He wasn't prepared to accept that their boss would deliberately sabotage her work.

If only Ace would let her go to the pits to check for herself! Unfortunately he'd been beyond reason, and after hearing in detail from Paul what a fiasco the whole performance had been she wasn't surprised. On present performance he was going to start way back on the grid unless the problem was sorted out; but she knew it would be. Jason Prior was going to come out of this shining like a knight in armour while she would be condemned to eternal darkness, everyone believing it was her fault.

Who was going to believe her? No one until Paul had finished checking her work, and she'd got the blend so right! Even the mechanics had been full of praise. She sighed. She had a pretty shrewd guess what Jason had done to have so altered the volatility but if she wasn't allowed down to the pits how would she ever prove it?

It wasn't really surprising therefore that she was wound tighter than a spring with suppressed energy as she waited for Ace to return. He'd threatened her with the direst reprisals if she dared to leave their suite, not guessing that wild horses wouldn't drag her away until she'd cleared the whole matter up. All the same when he did return she got a shock when she found he was accompanied by Mike and a complete stranger and that one side of Ace's face was bruised and swollen.

'Ace! What's happened? Did you crash?' He ignored her, walking past into his room followed by the stranger, who gave her a lop-sided grin. She turned to Mike, her face once more white with shock. He gave her a hard-eyed stare, then swung away to look out of the window.

'Mike, please?' He turned back to face her after

hearing her impassioned plea, but his mouth was grim.

'My God, what a day! First the fuel problems, and now this!'

'But what actually happened?'

'He slipped on a patch of oil trying to get away from Dara. Why that silly cow hasn't realised by now there is nothing doing as far as Ace is concerned God knows! Still, I don't suppose a high intelligence is one of her assets, and you have to give her ten out of ten for persistence. Miss Superglue has been following us around faithfully with a photographer in tow trying to immortalise their supposed passionate reunion. Well, Ace knocked that little idea flat but unfortunately himself as well as he hit his head on the door-frame trying to seek sanctuary in the pits.' He raised his eyes. 'Heaven preserve me from all women; they're nothing but a damned nuisance when they try to ensure my number-one driver is handicapped before the race has even started!'

He looked at her strained white face and continued impatiently, 'Look, you don't have to worry about Ace! That was Professor Adam Jenkinson that I brought with me. You must know he takes care of all the drivers' problems. We are lucky to have such an eminent man on call, and the drivers trust him absolutely as I'm sure you know.'

She smiled a little. 'He's damaged his eye, hasn't he? I know that can have serious consequences. . .'

'You mean a detached retina, quite apart from minor concussion, I suppose?' Mike laughed a little too heartily. 'We'll cross those bridges if we come to them, but in the meantime I hope we can count on your discretion?' She looked her surprise, and he continued impatiently, 'The Press, of course! There's nothing they'd like better than a drama like this just before the race, and don't think Dara or her escort will have kept their mouths shut!'

'I wouldn't dream of saying anything to them!' she responded indignantly. He gave her a cynical look, as much as to say that he only half believed her.

'Look, Ace is angry enough with me as it is, but if he thought I'd betray. . .' Kate left the sentence unfinished as she bit her lip.

'Why didn't you alert me that there was trouble between you and your boss? Jason tells me you've often made careless mistakes in your work, and that you've always resented him correcting you,' Mike enquired, and Kate knew from the way he spoke that he too blamed her for the trouble.

'I, too, find it incredible that anyone would go to the lengths he has just to discredit my work!' she answered bitterly. 'Oh, I know you won't believe me when I tell you that he doctored that fuel blend to make me look a fool, but one of the boys back in London knows; he's going to have my work independently checked before Jason gets home!'

'Oh, come on! Are you asking me to believe that he deliberately set out to sabotage your work?' Mike now looked distinctly disbelieving.

'Yes, exactly that!' she snapped. 'Anyway, it amazes me that none of you has apparently thought of comparing the print-outs of yesterday with today's work. If you'd done that you'd have seen at once there was a difference — the blend worked perfectly!'

Mike frowned back at her. 'Nobody's denying you did good work on that blend. It's just that you got careless. . .'

Kate stared back at him, her mouth set in a bitter line. 'I'm not careless, I never have been. . . And even if I'd made a mistake I'd be honest enough to admit it. Jason will sort out your problem, and you'll all think he's wonderful!' Her voice filled with scorn. 'But I'll tell you now, there are only three additives that could have had that effect on the car's perform-ance, and I'll write them down for you now.' She marched over to the desk set against the wall, and scribbled three chemical formulas on the hotel writing paper before folding it over and giving it to Mike.

'There! Get that checked and you'll find your problem. I'm fairly sure it's the first on the list. . . Jason'll string you a line, pretend to work flat out, but that'll be the answer he comes up with!' Her undeniable sincerity appeared to make Mike think.

'But it's crazy! If what you say is true he must know that the results would be checked?'

'But would you have bothered?' Kate again asked bitterly. 'No, I think it would have been easier just to take his word for it that I'd boobed, fallen down on the job. After all I'm only a girl, and not really important!' Her bitter sarcasm at last appeared to make Mike think again.

'I'll get this checked right away. If you're right I'll make sure IMP hear about it.'

'If you're honest you'll admit you're already half convinced!' she snapped back.

'OK, OK!' Mike threw his hands up in defeat. 'But if you've got any more surprises waiting to spring on us, then warn me about them now! Ace is my top driver, and you ought to know perfectly well there's a great deal riding on his shoulders at the moment. It's partly my job to ease the burden in any way I can. I don't blame him for falling for you, but don't you go giving him a hard time just before the race! He's going to need all his concentration to win, and I don't want to have to cope with any more off-track dramas. . .' He gave her a hard-eyed glance. 'Ace told me, by the way, that you're Eddie Ash's little sister. I have to admit that if I'd known that I wouldn't have asked to have you seconded to Carlisle Flint. . .'

Kate raised her chin to him, but she still couldn't stop the colour from flooding her cheeks. She longed, oh, she burned to be able to tell him the truth, but Ace's threats held; also by the way Mike was looking at her at the moment he probably wouldn't believe her if she told him the truth about their relationship. 'You needn't worry. I've always had better things to do with my time than to plot hypothetical revenge for something that happened ten years ago!' she snapped.

'I'm delighted to hear it,' Mike agreed, 'although after this latest little fracas you can't blame me for wondering, now can you?'

Kate was left speechless, but with a nasty sort of hollowness in her insides. It wasn't much fun being accused of something, and being unable to defend oneself.

'Now, if you'll excuse me, I'll join Adam and Ace to find out just exactly how much damage, thanks to you, he's suffered!'

'What do you mean "thanks to me"?' she protested.

'If you'd been around where you should have been, then possibly Ace wouldn't have had to take such instant action to avoid Dara!'

Kate's bitter yell of denial appeared to fall on deaf ears and she spun away on her heel, more than ready to take sanctuary in her own smaller room.

She threw herself angrily down on to the bed, furious at the predicament into which Jason had pitchforked her. For a time her emotions stopped her thinking clearly until she forced herself to concentrate on the problem logically. There seemed to be only one way to force Jason to leave her alone, and that had to be their employer IMP. A quick call to the personnel director Robert Dexter ought to bring advice and results.

Blessing the fact that there was a direct dialling code, she called London and was put through to Robert Dexter with commendable speed.

'Dr Ash? Hello, my dear, I'm so pleased you've called. . .' Kate was surprised to hear how relieved he sounded at hearing her voice.

'Mr Dexter, I'm afraid we've had a bit of a problem out here. . .'

'I already know about it, my dear, as does most of the world. I'm really sorry, but this has altered everything as far as our plans with you were concerned. I'm afraid the board thinks that in view of your now unacceptably high profile it would be better to — er — temporarily, of course, sever your connection with the company ——'

'What?' Kate interjected.

Robert Dexter obviously expected that shocked reaction because his voice sounded infinitely soothing, even formal. She noticed he called her by her title, not her Christian name.

'Please don't worry, Dr Ash. Financially you will be taken very good care of, I do assure you ——'

'Are you trying to tell me I've lost my job?' The rising tone of her voice emphasised her panic.

'I'm afraid that for the moment, yes, the company would prefer you to resign.'

'But why?' Kate wailed. 'Why should I be punished for what Jason Prior's tried to do to me ——?'

'As to that,' Robert Dexter broke in smoothly, 'the board feel, as I do, that Dr Prior no doubt had very good reason to doubt your ability to handle everything on your own. He's certainly had a long talk with me since you left the team ——'

'But that's nonsense!' Poor Kate sat up straight on her bed, her legs crossed beneath her, and tried to hang on to her sanity. 'You can't ask me to leave just because someone has blackened my name ——'

Once more she was interrupted. 'I'm afraid we can, my dear. Look, we are all very sorry, but we have to think of the company's good name. No one is ever going to believe you are totally innocent over this, and the sort of publicity the fuel blend failure attracted this afternoon is extremely damaging, as I'm sure you are aware. Please don't worry about your finances. A package is already being worked out for you by our legal department which should soften the blow considerably, and after all there has been no lasting query raised against the quality of your work; the suggestion that your ideas need checking——'

'No query being raised against my work? Oh, yes, there has! Asked to leave because one of your employees was jealous of my ideas and set out to make me fall guy. No! You can't expect me to take the blame for it! I hardly call that fair.'

'As I've already said, we now believe Dr Prior's version of the facts.'

'But I told you when I came to see you that day. That was the first time I had any idea!'

'Well, if that's so it is indeed a great pity, Dr Ash, but in view of Dr Prior's importance to the company you must understand that we have little choice in this matter. It's been a very unfortunate episode for all concerned.'

'You can say that again!'

'I myself am flying out this evening with my wife to join the IMP team.'

'Thanks a bunch! And what am I supposed to do? Stay locked in my room?'

'That's not such a bad idea, Dr Ash. The Press interest in this affair seems likely to reach ludicrous heights with the Grand Prix tomorrow. I think it would be extremely prudent of you to keep a very low profile indeed for the next few days.'

'I'm not going to accept that! I want you and the company to find some way to get me out of this mess

I've been landed in. How am I supposed to do my job tomorrow, for heaven's sake? You'll have to sort something out otherwise I too might give a Press conference so the world can hear my side of the story!'

'I don't think that would be a very wise move to make, Dr Ash. I suggest you let Ace Barton guide you over this. He at least has experience of dealing with the Press and the company have already allocated another member of the team for tomorrow's race.'

'It's so unfair!' she wailed. 'I've lost my job just because Jason Prior was frightened I might get the chance to take over his fairly soon. Why haven't you checked with the others on the team? I've probably lost all future chances of gaining anything comparable ever again. Oh, what's the use. . .?' She dropped the phone back on its hook and rolled back on to the bed, her eyes tight shut.

She wanted to scream with the hopelessness of it all, the unfairness, but she knew there was nothing she could do. A minor research chemist like herself hadn't a hope of fighting a large multi-national like IMP. She lay back, her body rigid, as she reviewed the last few catastrophic days of her life. Her thoughts crystallised with the suddenness of a bolt of lightning. She sat up. It had all happened because Ace Barton had tried to play God in her life, and she'd let him get away with it. Before he'd interfered in her life she had been part of a team, doing a job that she enjoyed well.

In a flash she was off her bed and on her way to

have it out with the one man responsible. It was the sight of the stranger, the professor, that stopped her in her tracks. So single-minded had she been that she'd forgotten the presence of Mike and this man. She had stopped so suddenly that he obviously thought he'd distressed her.

'Don't worry! Ace's eye will be fine. . . There's no concussion or any other sign of injury apart from the bruising! We're going to have to work hard to keep the swelling down, but as long as he can see out of both eyes tomorrow morning I shall be quite happy to pronounce him fit!'

Kate had been so taken up with her own affairs that she'd rather forgotten Ace's part in the drama. 'Oh! Well, that's good. . .' she replied a little inadequately.

'I don't think we've met, have we?' he queried, coming forward with an outstretched hand.

'Kate — er — Kate Ash,' she mumbled.

'Adam Jenkinson at your service! You're going to have the job of changing the ice-packs for me through the night, aren't you?'

'Me?' Kate looked slightly horrified.

'Yes. Mike and I agree that the fewer people who see Ace at present the better! By tomorrow the swelling will have gone down considerably, you know. With a little judicious handling to hide the worst of the bruising, I think we'll manage to minimise the impact it will have on the Press. I understand you've very wisely opted to stay out of the limelight. Quite right! By the time we get to Jerez hopefully most of the fuss will have died down. Now,

I must be on my way. I've left instructions by the bed, but Mike'll be back later.' With a last, quizzical look at her slightly stunned expression, he waited for Mike to join him, then both men walked out of the suite, leaving her alone with Ace.

Ace. She lifted her chin and walked into his room prepared to do battle. He was lying on the large double bed with the first of the ice-packs over one side of his face. One blue eye swivelled in her direction, but his head didn't move.

'Come to look at your revenge?'

'If you think that's my revenge then you've certainly repaid the compliment, haven't you?' she hissed. The blue eye looked a little uncertain as she leant over the bed, her face pale with suppressed anger.

'What's the matter?' he enquired, obviously unhappy to have her looming over him like some avenging goddess.

'Nothing you'd consider particularly important. Just that I happen to have lost my job!'

'Oh! So IMP have given you the push, have they? Well, I can't say I'm particularly surprised. This is not the sort of publicity they enjoy. You really blew it today.'

Kate deliberately let all control go, let her anger at this man rip through her with all the force of a forest fire.

'I just wish to God I'd never met you!' She leant lower over the bed, to give her words extra emphasis, but Ace took immediate and unfair advantage of her low centre of gravity, and pulled her down on to him, his two arms holding her firmly pressed against his full length.

'That's better!' One blue eye had narrowed with laughter. 'This is the best way I know to sort out problems, and it looks as if you and I certainly need to have our minds distracted! Mike tells me that there is a remote possibility we may have misjudged you after all, so why don't you try spinning me this fairy-tale?'

'Let me go this instant!' Furiously Kate tried to wriggle herself free until she was warned quite unmistakably that Ace found her movements provocatively exciting. The thin cotton of their clothes could not hide their bodies' warmth from each other, and she became aware of a curious lassitude that seemed intent on relaxing her tense muscles.

'No way! You owe me, Kate. . .' He spoke lazily, slowly. 'I've got to lie here for the next twelve hours without moving with an ice-pack over half my face because you walked out and left me to the mercy of a predatory pit-popsy!' Intent on trying not to forget what had brought her marching into his room, she tried to stoke the fading embers of her rage.

'And if you hadn't interfered and ruined my life I might not now have my career in ruins! I've been publicly blamed for letting the team down—vilified by the Press! What do you think my family are going to say to me now? I wouldn't be surprised if my father refused to talk to me!'

'You blame me?' His hold on her had slackened slightly, but she didn't feel sure he'd let her escape

without an undignified fight, so she didn't push her
luck.

'Who else?' Her brown eyes blazed with indignation. The warmth of his body, his cradling arms,
were still having their softening effect on her physically, so she tried even harder to whip up her rage
and indignation.

'You're incredibly naïve about my sex, aren't you?'
His mouth was tilted in a narrow, exciting smile.
'You think by rushing in here breathing fire and fury
you will distract me from pursuing other matters. . .'

That was it. That really lit the fuse. Kate shut her
eyes and screamed until he let her go.

'Sssh, Kate! For heaven's sake. . .'

She knelt next to him, her hands beating furiously
on the mattress. 'I'd have told you!' she shouted. 'I
told Mike, I told Robert Dexter. Why won't any of
you believe me?' Her brown eyes now had a film of
tears over them. 'Do you really believe I'd have
blown a career I loved just to get even with you for
something that happened ten years ago? You think
like all the rest. Just because I'm a girl I can be
brushed aside as if I'm of no account. You chose to
believe a stinking little rat who can't take the fact
that a woman might just be better at his job than he
is!'

'Then you'd better tell me!' Ace had sat up and
discarded the ice-pack so that he could face her. So
once again she told her story.

'I think he sent me out to France,' she finished,
'hoping I'd make a mess of things. When it became
clear I was a success he tried to get rid of me

permanently. When that didn't work he cooked up this present plan. . .' She looked at his expression, which was ambivalent to say the least.

'Why is it so difficult for everyone to believe me?' she demanded through clenched teeth. 'I don't tell lies. . .'

'I suppose it's feasible that a girl with your looks and brains could drive someone to behave in the way you've described. Perhaps you really wounded his pride when you turned him down so he wants to see you humiliated.' He gave her a searching stare, then outlined the contours of her face with one finger. 'Of course what people find impossible to understand about you is that you genuinely don't know what effect you have on men.'

There was no denying his words had a soothing effect, but she didn't want to be soothed, she wanted him to accept her version of events. Even so she found it impossible to keep her mind properly on her own problems when he continued to look at her like that, so she picked him up on one niggling point that continued to irritate her.

'Why do you keep on saying I'm inexperienced? How do you know?' Kate was in such a state that she didn't really know what she was asking.

'This is how I know. . .' Ace once more pulled her down next to him, and his lips found hers. Tantalisingly, teasing, with feather-light touches of his tongue, he gently forced from her a response, and she was lost.

Tenderly her fingertips traced the swelling around his eye as she surrendered totally to the moment.

Just for this once, she told herself, she wasn't prepared to fight her body's response, and the intensity
of her desire rose as she allowed him to pull her close
to his warm maleness.

It was madness, yes—a crazy, upside-down
response to her turbulent emotions earlier, but her
logical mind was slowly disintegrating under the
wealth of feelings and emotions she'd tried to keep
hidden for so long.

She buried herself in the scent of him, and the last
traces of control were lost as his hands started to
explore the round fullness of her breasts. Slowly,
gently, he eased off her T-shirt and she smiled with
pleasure as his breath was sharply exhaled at the
sight of her semi-nakedness.

She rubbed sinuously against him as she felt a deep
thrill at his arousal, and shut her eyes as he removed
the last fragile barrier. She couldn't control a moan
of delight as his lips caught and teased her sensitive
nipples. Wave after wave of sensation ran through
her until she thought she might drown in a tide of
pleasure as his tongue and hands explored the soft
silkiness of her body, his lips always returning,
though, to meet her lips, like a humming-bird seeking nectar.

Every nerve filled with tingling life, she let him
teach her new sensations, new feelings, totally passive under his expert touch, until she too began to
know the need to feel his skin under her fingers.
Wantonly she twisted her arms around his neck,
revelling in the great shudder of desire she felt in
response, but with surprise she quickly became aware

that he was holding back, almost as if he was having second thoughts.

'Love me, Ace. . .' she whispered in his ear, painfully trying to keep hold of that insubstantial thread of feeling before it evaporated between them.

'Kate, Kate. . . Gently, sweetheart! I'm not sure you're ready; you might regret——' But she didn't allow him to finish, her mouth seeking his, her tongue shyly exploring its hot depths. She didn't want to hear any words. All she wanted was to feel, to bring this overwhelming sensation of physical pleasure to its logical conclusion. Nothing else was allowed to matter as her pent-up feelings were released, leaving her rocking on a sea of pleasure of such width and depth that she was totally out of control and overwhelmed.

'Kate! We shouldn't be doing this, but. . . Oh, God! I'd have to be a saint to stop. . .'

'Don't you want me?' she growled innocently looking up into eyes now slate-blue and heavy-looking with unsated sex.

'I want you. . .' She felt the surge of power in his body. 'Oh, yes, I've wanted you from that first meeting in France.' His fingers were tracing a path down her spine that sent delicious tremors through her body.

'So. . .?' Her eyes looked absurdly dark, like hidden pools, half hidden by that bright curtain of hair to the watching man.

He gave a great sigh. 'But I'm not going to take you; not tonight. . .'

To start with she found it difficult to take in, to

appreciate the meaning of his words. He was reject-
ing her. It couldn't, it shouldn't be happening, but it
was. . . Her worst nightmare had come true. She'd
offered herself to him, offered her girlish hopes and
dreams, everything she'd kept bottled up for ten
years. All of her sweet, loving nature that she'd
turned in on herself, waiting for this one moment in
her life, this moment of truth, and it had all been for
nothing.

Shocked, frightened, and more than half scared by
the desolation that threatened to consume her, she
slid away from him.

'Kate?' He half sat up and put out a hand as if to
touch her, aware that something traumatic had
occurred.

'Leave me alone!' she whispered.

'What is it? What's the matter?'

She shut her eyes in anguish. How could he ask
that? What was he, some kind of sadist?

'Do you really want to humiliate me any further?'
The bitter sarcasm in her voice stopped him.

'Kate, you idiot! You don't understand. . .' He sat
up on the bed, and she saw him wince.

'You'd better keep quiet if you want to race
tomorrow,' she told him, still in that cold little voice.
'I'm leaving, getting out. You can apply to my father
for money if you still want to punish him for not
backing you. I don't care any more.' With one fluid
movement she reached down on the bed and picked
up her T-shirt, putting it on.

'You're forgetting something. . .' Ace held up the
black lace provocatively by its straps, almost as if

with humour he could defuse the situation between them.

'Keep it to remind you of the time when Eddie's little sister wasn't good enough for you!' She whirled round then and left the room, banging the door behind her, ignoring his cry of her name.

As she walked into the big sitting-room, Mike Booker walked into the suite again. His eyes took in her obvious dishevelment with slight embarrassment.

'I'm sorry,' he stuttered slightly, 'I'll come back later.'

'Don't bother to go. I'm the one who's leaving.' Her voice sounded clipped, rather staccato, and it seemed not properly to belong to her any more. 'I want out, Mike. I don't care how you arrange it, but do it. If you won't, I'll do it myself!'

The bedroom door swung open to reveal Ace, now holding the ice-pack back to his face.

'Are you mad?' It was Mike's turn to take charge. 'For heaven's sake go back and lie down. You heard what the prof said. . .'

'Kate?' Ace turned towards her.

'I should do what the man said.' Coldly, calmly, she walked towards her room and walked in, so carefully shutting the door after her that it was more of a controlled insult than any violent bang to the two men still watching.

The next afternoon found Kate lying on a lounger beside a pool in the Algarve. Her bright hair was hidden under a sunhat, and she was disguised with dark glasses, but no one had shown the slightest interest in her. Mike had managed to smuggle her out of the hotel yesterday evening, but, as he had pointed out to her, it would be impossible to get out of the country at the moment without alerting the Press.

So this two bedroomed apartment in a hotel complex had been borrowed from some golfing friend of Mike's, and here she was to stay until Mike could get her back home to London.

She lay, tense and unrelaxed, soaking up the surprising strength of the autumn sun while the Portuguese Grand Prix was run on the testing Estoril track. Her ears weren't full of the gentle chat of the middle-aged golf widows working on their tans while their husbands perfected their game. She was miles away, her internal ears full of the roar of the Formula One engines as they screamed their way around the seventy testing, bumpy laps.

There was a television in the apartment, but Kate had resolutely disciplined herself against turning it on. She was finished with motor racing, she told herself fiercely, but she couldn't help feeling empty and lost inside, as if an important part of her had been amputated.

She spent most of her time telling herself that it was the loss of her job that was so catastrophic; it had nothing to do with Ace Barton. But the wound was still so sore and tender that she could hardly bear to think about it. Each time her unruly thoughts returned to the fiasco, the pain became worse. She tried to tell herself it was her pride that had been damaged, but something raw and bleeding inside told a different story.

In the end she wasn't able to resist the temptation to find out, to know. Forcing herself to walk slowly back to the apartment, she turned on the TV to catch the final closing stages of the race. Of course Ace was OK, she told herself. He wouldn't be allowed to race if his eye was bad, but she knew only too well what a punishing endurance it was for the drivers. The physical discomfort of the cars, the intense concentration required to push the parameters that bit further, the G-force that racked their bodies.

Ace was running third, his team-mate ahead of him, their closest opposition in the lead. Kate wasn't surprised; yesterday must have taken its toll even though he was superlatively fit. She guessed that, whatever had been done to minimise the damage, he'd have a headache by now, and she couldn't stop herself feeling an immediate pang of sympathy.

She guessed that Mike Booker would be calling curses down on her head because he'd been hoping a one-two win at Estoril would clinch the constructors' championship for Carlisle Flint, quite apart from putting Ace into an unbeatable lead. It was impossible for her not to feel hard-done-by as she watched. Would she ever feel able to accept that motor racing was no longer a major part of her life?

The line-up didn't change as they crossed the chequered flag, and Kate turned the TV off, not feeling able to watch the award-winning ceremony. She knew there were things she should be trying to sort out in her life, but she didn't want to face up to certain ideas that lurked at the back of her mind.

The apartment was self-catering, or one could eat

in one of the hotel restaurants. Kate, still frightened
she might be recognised, had chosen to have meals
sent up to the apartment from the nearest retaurant.
She hadn't dared to explore outside the confines of
the hotel's extensive grounds. She was beginning to
be more than a bit worried about the expenses
involved in her escape, and hoped it wouldn't be too
long before she could escape back to anonymity and
London.

After a frugal meal, she wrapped herself in a long
white cashmere cardigan that Ace had insisted on
buying her, and sat out on the balcony that over-
looked the distant Atlantic ocean, and, more
immediately, the beautiful gardens of the hotel. Her
thoughts were sad and for once she didn't try to
correct their melancholic turn. A CD of Dire Straits'
greatest hits she'd found in the apartment matched
her mood as she looked out into the dark night, lit
only by the dramatic outside lighting of the gardens.

Ace was so much part of her unacknowledged
dreams that it was barely a shock therefore to find
herself pulled up and into his strong arms. A least
that was what she told herself afterwards to excuse
her instinctive response to his lips.

'Ah, my Kate! This is the best reward of all. . .'
His voice sounded husky and more than a little tired,
but it brought her back to the present with painful
clarity.

'What are you doing here? Let me go!' She began
to fight for her freedom, bitter thoughts knifing
through her.

'For God's sake, Kate, stop it! I've been through enough today. . .'

'You've been through enough! Oh, lord. . .' She turned away from him back into the big sitting-room, wondering how she was to bear this fresh indignity without giving her innermost secret away.

Ace followed her, prudently shutting the big sliding glass doors after him for more privacy. Kate turned, like an animal at bay. 'Having second thoughts on what you missed out on last night?' she sneered.

He closed his eyes, and she couldn't help but see how appallingly tired he looked. 'How did you get here?' she whispered. 'You didn't drive?'

The brilliant blue of his eyes caught and held hers. 'No, no. . . Only from Faro airport. I flew down by helicopter from Estoril.'

'You're mad. . . Aren't you exhausted?'

'I'm tired, yes, but I wasn't prepared to leave you labouring under your misapprehensions any longer than I had to. . .' There was a small silence. 'I didn't make love to you last night, not because I didn't want to, but because it wasn't the right time, or place. Also, once we started I'd find it very hard to stop, and you may perhaps have forgotten I was due to race today?' A slight smile quivered the ends of his mouth, and if one eye looked slightly more narrow than the other there wasn't much obvious bruising.

'You deserved better than a one-night stand, Kate. I've been trying to fight my need for you, but last night proved one thing to me—you and I are dynamite together. Mentally we both might have reservations about each other, but physically there are no barriers between us, are there?'

Mesmerised, Kate shook her head, unable to deny to him the truth of his words.

'I want us to continue where we left off, Kate. I think if we do that we might both discover that we can give each other a great deal of pleasure.'

The picture that his words conjured up left her breathless, but another, stronger part of her was screaming in denial. She shook her head.

'No, Ace, you've got it the wrong way round. It won't work between us until we resolve our problems. You don't trust me, and I. . .well, let's just say I still have reservations about you.'

'What happened to your reservations last night?' he sneered. 'I didn't notice you having any then. . . Why, you were as hot for me as I was for you!'

It was Kate's turn to shut her eyes. 'I know,' she whispered. 'That's why I left. . .'

'You want to turn your back on what could be so great between us?' She heard the incredulity in his voice and it fuelled the small truth that had been niggling at her, unacknowledged, all day.

'I want more than physical love!' she told him baldly. 'An affair with you is never going to be enough for me.'

His face settled into a remote yet also slightly calculating expression.

'Are you expecting me to offer you a permanent

commitment when we don't even know each other properly?'

She heard the amazement, as if what she'd suggested had to be beyond all rational consideration; certainly not anything that had ever merited any thought on his part.

'So you thought I'd be content to be your girlfriend, your mistress?' she enquired, her face blank. 'For as long as it suited you?'

Infuriatingly his expression remained enigmatic, but Kate refused to be diverted. 'I'm sorry to disappoint you, Ace, but I'm afraid that deal doesn't interest me!' It hurt her to lie, because she'd always been so truthful all her life.

'Don't twist my arm, Kate! I've never liked being forced into a decision.'

'I'm not forcing you into anything, Ace. I'm just telling you my thoughts, trying to put across my point of view for a change. I've a perfect right to my feelings. You've already done immense damage to my life. Why should I give you *carte blanche* to continue?'

He looked at her unyielding face, and something seemed to give in his own as he gave way to frustration and bad temper, let alone physical exhaustion.

'You calculating little bitch! Why, I bet you never had the slightest intention of following through last night, did you? If I hadn't called a halt, you'd have engineered one somehow. . . It wouldn't surprise me to hear you'd planned this all along. You wanted me on a string so you could play cat to my mouse. . .

My God, what a fool I've been!' The blue eyes had
narrowed dangerously. 'Now you've lost your job
through your ex-boss's devious manipulations I suppose you decided to try to move in permanently on
me! I'm now going to teach you a long-overdue
lesson, my dear. This is what happens when you
drive a man too far!'

CHAPTER SIX

ACE reached for her, his mouth closing over hers, denying her any chance to protest. Kate tried to turn her head away, but he held her head steady with one hand twisted lightly in her hair. Already he had managed to force a response from her, as her lips parted to let his darting tongue tease yet further weakness into her limbs.

Expertly his hands began their slow, feverish exploration of her bare skin, tormenting as they sought to inflame her further and further so that she forgot everything but the pleasure he could bring her.

Her nipples had become rigid, almost unbearably sensitised, as his fingers gently squeezed and played with her firm round breasts. She was hardly aware of him stripping her of her clothes before his tongue started its own journey of exploration. She was quite unable to control the groan that rose in her throat.

He stopped then, and picked her up, shouldering his way into the bedroom with the large double bed already turned down for the night. The feeling of cool linen sheets against her heated skin just added to the almost unbearable sexual tension she was feeling. He stripped off the rest of her clothes, then took off his own, all the time feasting his eyes on her nakedness before lying down next to her.

125

She knew it was wrong, but she couldn't stop herself feeling exquisite pleasure as she watched the brilliant blue eyes explore her hot nakedness. Quite unable to stop herself, she too reached out to stroke the satin-softness of his skin, her eyes darkening as she saw the many bruises that came from trying to control the incredibly fast cars that flew so low and hard round the Grand Prix circuits.

She felt him quiver with pleasure at her tentative touch, so concentrated with a single-minded fervour on trying to give him as much provocative excitement as he was giving her, striving always to find more and more sensitive places.

Ace made love to her in a silence made all the more potent when her roving caresses forced him to respond with a groan of pleasure as they touched each other intimately.

All Kate's previous sexual experience had been limited to clumsy caresses which she'd had no difficulty in resisting. In fact she'd always doubted her own sensuality until Ace had awoken it so expertly. She'd had no idea that she was capable of behaving in such a passionate way, or of forgetting all her inhibitions so completely.

His chest was sleekly well muscled, with few dark hairs to ruffle its warm, silky perfection, and she enjoyed running the palms of her hands over it, teasing his own nipples into hardness. Dark hair at his waist narrowed excitingly, inviting her questing hands to explore lower. She felt a deep, sensual pleasure as she held his leaping, quivering manhood in check, but the heat of him was so dangerously exciting that she arched herself in mute supplication, begging him to give her the release that her body craved.

He parted her thighs fiercely, and she moaned as his head sank, his tongue driving her to a frenzy.

'Please, oh, please. . .'

He took pity on her, driving himself inside her so deeply, her virginity causing him only momentary check. Wild exultation at having him so close made sure her momentary pain was no more than that, as he slipped easily into the rhythm that had her half sobbing with delight until his voice joined her own.

She couldn't stop the tears of happiness that slid from her closed eyes, as her body, still quiveringly alive, shuddered gently to a stop; over-excited nerves twitched into the deepest peace she'd ever known. They drew away from each other, so mutually sated with explosive body contact that both needed a temporary reprieve. She felt him collapse next to her, knowing that, exhausted as he was, he would sink into immediate and deep sleep, and, secure that he would still be there in the morning, she too, sank into slumber. Her last waking thought had been that she was wrong, and that Ace had been right all the time.

She awoke with her body lazily relaxed, only slight soreness to remind her of what had happened the previous night. She stretched with remembered delight, then turned to look at the man lying so quietly next to her.

Vivid blue eyes met hers in a question.

'Good morning.' There was a definite query on the first word, and she half smiled in return.

'Good morning, Ace. . .'

They lay there, their bodies not quite touching, Kate fighting hard to contain the feelings that seemed to be once more racing out of control. Beneath the overwhelming memories of physical delight there were fears—a fear that she might not have measured up in some way. After all, she wasn't ever likely to forget his first damning exposé of her character, was she? There was also fear that he was going to punish her in some unpleasant way for Jason's actions, and other, deeper fears that even now she refused to acknowledge.

'You have a very expressive face. What's bothering you?'

Her eyes flew up to meet his in a panic until she screwed up sufficient courage to put her fear into words.

'You told me, at Paul Ricard, that I was. . . I was empty——'

He interrupted, his voice husky. 'I was wrong.'

Once more her eyes flew to meet his, but this time there was a shy pleasure in their brown depths until again a shadow darkened them.

'Now what?' His face was non-committal, and Kate felt suddenly shy because of the wave of lust that swept over her as she looked back at his unshaven cheeks.

'I. . .oh, nothing. . .'

'Do you regret what happened last night?'

'No! How could I?'

He let out his breath in a gentle sigh of air. 'Then

forget whatever it is, Kate, because it couldn't be important. . .' One hand stretched out to cup one side of her face, the other slid under her waist to draw her close to him. 'This is the only thing that matters at the moment between us, isn't it?' His voice deepened, and Kate felt herself melt in response as his heated body at last touched hers again.

Later, much later, they breakfasted out on the balcony with only the Portuguese gardeners near by to disturb their peace.

'How was the race yesterday?' Kate asked idly, striving for at least a semblance of normality between them.

'Not too good,' was the response. 'IMP changed the mix.'

'Who changed it? Why?' Kate looked up, her attention now well and truly caught. Ace shrugged.

'The fuel technician decided the burn wasn't right. . .'

'Jason?' she asked.

He gave her a quick glance. 'Yes. I wondered at the time because it *was* professional jealousy after all, I suppose.'

It was Kate's turn to shrug, but Ace saw that she looked a little distressed.

'It's crazy that he even refused to use my blend when he must have known it was working well. . .'

Ace heard the unspoken bitterness behind the words, but he didn't comment on it.

'Mike and I had already decided to go back to Blend Six for Jerez if it's still hot.'

Her eyes blazed back at him as she fought to

contain her inner excitement. 'Ace, can you get me copies of the print-outs?'

He gave her a reluctant grin. 'So you're still interested in the business, then?'

'Why ask? You know I am!' She made no pretence of hiding her eagerness, and he gave her a wry smile.

'Mike thrust them at me before I left, so I brought them with me. I imagine he hoped you'd look at them. We don't want to mess up the next meeting, now do we?'

Kate looked at him, her eyes suddenly worried. 'They've asked me to resign, Ace. I can't do it; it's unethical.'

'But you haven't done so yet, have you? And if you don't resign then there's no reason for you not to continue to act as adviser to Carlisle Flint. Apart from anything else you're seconded to our team now so asking you to leave isn't entirely up to IMP any more.'

'You're forgetting something. Mike doesn't seem to want me around!'

'Oh, yes, he does! Robert Dexter flew home with Prior last night and Carlisle Flint have gone on record saying that they are not interested in a change of team. IMP are going to have to accept that you're still their on-the-spot representative. Anyway, I think Dexter has realised that asking you to resign was a mistake. Prior admitted to the world at large on TV that the disappointing race was partly his fault and nothing to do with you. He went on to admit that IMP's golden girl, as the Press have dubbed you, is a brilliant young chemist in her own right!'

'Who twisted his arm to make him admit that?' she demanded incredulously.

'Mike. With a little help from me as well.'

Kate was silent as she digested this fact.

'I still don't believe he wants me around!' Her eyes were accusing. 'You told him about Eddie.'

'He had to know, Kate. Don't you know that by now the Press will have dug up everything they can about your past?'

'My past? Of course they won't bother!'

But Ace could see that she didn't sound or look as totally convinced as her words.

'I'm afraid they will. Somebody'll make the connection with Eddie — you can be sure of that.'

'So what do you want me to do?'

'I'm afraid we've neither of us much choice. I've got to work pretty intensely with the team, and we need you as well. Don't worry about Jason; IMP have promised there won't be a repeat performance, but you'll have to work with your colleagues. Will that cause problems for you?'

'No, it shouldn't do.'

'Good! Well, much as I'd love to stay on here, I'm afraid it isn't going to be feasible. So tomorrow it's back to work, but for the rest of today we have no one to please but each other.' His voice sounded lazily relaxed, but his eyes, in spite of the smile, were giving her such exciting messages that Kate, under his spell as never before, could feel her heart once more begin to beat with a heavy, sensuous rhythm.

* * *

Kate was down in the pit lane for the Friday qualifying session, her nerves nearly as wound up as the drivers', knowing that Ace was waiting to live up to his name with the fastest lap. In many ways this moment was infinitely more exciting than the actual race itself because these qualifying laps asked so much from car and driver. As he pulled out of the pit lane for the first time she found it hard to keep her emotions second to her job. The number-two car with Dino Tremiti had done well and held current pole position, but even if Ace did brilliantly the Brazilian who drove for Carlisle Flint's closest rivals was hot on his tail, and he had a reputation for being able to go just that little bit faster under the pressure of a time to beat.

Act returned, having done a good time, but not quite good enough, and he knew it. Kate and a couple of her team-mates from IMP were waiting for him, and he shook his head at them.

'The burn isn't right. I'm losing power on the straights, and the three of you had better work at it because I've only got one more chance!'

'What about the set-up?' Mike queried.

'The set-up's fine. We've still got a fuel problem, that's all!' He gave Kate and her companions a brooding, sarcastic look before turning away from them to talk at length with Mike and the mechanics.

'Hey! I thought he was supposed to be your boyfriend,' Jim Connor, one of the fuel technicians, laughed at her.

'As you can see Ace Barton gets his priorities in the proper order. Getting the car right is far more

important than any girlfriend at this moment,' Kate
answered, her brow already furrowed as she studied
the print-outs of the car's performance.

'Don't you mind?' Stan, the other member of
IMP's team, asked slyly.

'No, why should I?' She looked up, surprise on
her face. 'He's absolutely right, and if we don't get
our act together he's likely to be a great deal more
forceful next time round!' That shut them up, she
thought with a wry smile, although why they should
be so surprised at her reaction was another puzzle.
She was here to do a job, and doing her job properly
entailed keeping her personal feelings strictly under
control. She expected no favours from Ace, and he
would be the last to give her any as far as her job
was concerned.

All the same it wasn't easy to stop herself from
wondering if he too was having difficulties in not
remembering what had happened over the last forty-
eight hours. She shook her head fiercely, then concentrated entirely on her present work.

All the same, the day of the race Ace was third on
the grid, Dino Tremiti ahead of him, but pole was
taken by his greatest rival. The Press were openly
speculating that if his rival won, then the world
championship would be wide open for the last two
races on the calendar.

Ace had retreated from Kate, and she was made
painfully aware that his reservations about her had
grown in proportion to her failure to find out why his
car was under-performing.

She and her two companions worked half the night

in trying to come up with an answer, but as Dino's car was working perfectly they were forced to the conclusion that the problem did not lie in their department, even though this was fiercely disputed by the rest of the Carlisle Flint team.

As Kate looked into Ace's narrowed, unforgiving eyes before the race, she knew that, unfair or not, he held her somehow responsible, and his last words to her bore that out.

'You won't stop me winning, you know!' The mockery couldn't disguise the aggressive determination which chilled her to the bone.

'Take care,' she whispered back, frightened by the sheer naked will to succeed that she surprised on his face.

'Frightened something might happen to me?' he sneered. 'No chance. My name's not Eddie Ash!'

The extreme cruelty of his words threw her totally off balance, so much so that she lost all colour, as, half dizzy, she turned away to hide her shock.

'Kate!' One hand grabbed her wrist. She felt sick, even though there was no skin contact between them as he was already wearing his inner cotton gloves.

'Good luck, Ace. . .' She couldn't bring herself to look at him, and God knew how she managed to drag out the conventional words in a voice already husky with pain.

'Look, I didn't mean. . . I'm sorry. . .'

'Forget it!' She turned to allow her eyes to meet his, and, at their expression, he swore deeply.

'Ace, Ace!' Mike's voice, commanding, imperative, had him reluctantly obeying its uncompromising call as he ran lightly back to sit in the car in readiness to leave the pits and take his place on the grid.

Kate looked round rather blindly to find her colleagues, and, having located them, wasted little time. 'I've got a really bad headache. . . I'm afraid you'll have to manage without me. . .'

'You look awful!' Stan told her. 'Are you going back to the hotel?'

'No. I'll be in the motor home. I've got some pills. If I take them now, and lie down, I should be OK in a couple of hours.'

'Just in time to wake up for the finish! OK, Kate, don't worry. Don't forget we've both done this a hell of a lot more times than you have!' It was impossible for Stan to hide the fact that he was pleased she wasn't going to be around, and Kate accepted that here indeed was yet another male chauvinist jealous and unhappy at having his territory invaded by a woman. Not feeling up to arguing the point, she left quietly, knowing everyone else in the Carlisle Flint team was wound up as tight as the drivers, waiting for the green light.

She took the pills and lay down to rest with her eyes closed. She heard the noise of the start but not even that had the power to disturb her thoughts, which were totally turned inwards on to herself.

She'd been such an idiot, hadn't she? Why, almost right from the start she'd known she was playing with fire, and the rest of the cliché was proving to be disastrously right.

What she'd known instinctively from the start was absolutely right. She should never have allowed

herself to become emotionally involved with a man
who so patently distrusted her. It wasn't IMP's fault,
or hers, that he had started at Jerez in third position,
but she'd been a convenient whipping-boy for his
suspicions.

These last heady hours in his arms had proved a
chimera, a mirage after all. Their relationship wasn't
built on solid foundations, so it was hardly surprising,
was it, that it should collapse at the first sign of
trouble?

But I love him! Unacknowledged before, the truth
fought to the surface of her mind, demanding recognition. He was difficult to live with, impossibly single-
minded over his career, yet none of that seemed to
matter as she balanced the weight of her new discov-
ery against all she knew of him.

We could be happy, I know we could! part of
herself cried out. If only he'd give us a chance. . .
But the darker side of her nature rose up cynically to
rebut her hopes. He's into sex, but he's never once
mentioned love. . . He doesn't trust you, and probably never will, and that's all your own fault!

Her head turned restlessly on the pillow as she
strove to distance herself from the increasingly
excited voice of the commentator and the air-splitting
whine of the high-revving engines.

The pain in her head had subsided into the background, but she felt it was still dangerously capable
of moving once again into the foreground if she got
up. So she lay still, her eyes shut, as her thoughts
jumbled ceaselessly around her mind.

'Kate?' A gentle tap on the door.

'Yes?' She risked half sitting up. One of the PR girls walked in.

'Oh, lord! Have you got a migraine? I'm sorry, I shouldn't have disturbed you.'

'It's OK, it's just a bad headache. What is it, Mary? Has there been an accident?'

'No, no, nothing like that! The race is going great. . . Look, the office has just had a call from your father. He wants to talk to you.'

'My father?' Kate sat up fully, her attention now totally concentrated.

'Yes, he's back at the hotel.'

'My father? Here in Jerez?'

'Yes. Do you want to talk?'

'I'd better. . .' Kate tried to clear her head. What on earth could her father be doing out here? If he'd come for the race. . . But no, that didn't make sense, otherwise he wouldn't be at the hotel. . . She tried to clear her mind of any fuzziness, as she followed Mary outside towards the other motor home which was used as an office and for corporate hospitality.

'Daddy?' She sounded tense, and a little disbelieving that she was actually going to talk to her father.

'Katharine. I'm pleased I've managed to get hold of you at last. Listen, have you got to stay on at the track, or is it possible for you to leave and come back to the hotel?'

'Well, I suppose I could get away, but Daddy—why?'

'I think that'll be better answered when we're alone together. So I can expect you when?'

'About twenty minutes? I'll have to see if I can borrow a car.'

'Good. I'll be waiting in the lobby.' He rang off.

Kate managed to persuade one of the drivers of the hire cars Carlisle Flint had laid on for sponsors to drop her back to the hotel where the team were based. The driver was enthusiastically following the race on his radio, but Kate, whose knowledge of Spanish was negligible, allowed it all to flow by her. For once her interest was not centred on the Grand Prix, but on her father, and his reasons for coming out to Spain to find her.

When he stood up to greet her in the lobby of the hotel, her heart contracted a little with love. He looked so much older now his hair was grey, but for all that he was still a distinguished-looking man.

'Katharine.' He gave her a cold kiss on the cheek. He'd never shortened her name, or been a demonstrative man, and she still found it almost impossible to guess what he was thinking.

'It's lovely to see you, Daddy, but why didn't you let me know earlier? I could have got you tickets for the Grand Prix.'

'I thought you'd understood that my interest in Grand Prix racing had died with your brother.'

'Well, yes, but why are you here?'

The lobby of the hotel was virtually deserted, nearly everyone of consequence either at the track for the race, or having their siesta.

'I should have thought you could guess that quite easily as well. . .' He looked at her under frowning brows. 'Your mother has been very upset indeed by all the publicity about you and Ace Barton.'

'Oh. . .' Kate felt herself gripped by a familiar chill. Her father was cross with her, if not downright angry, and she felt like weeping inside. It wouldn't do to cry in front of him. He'd beaten that habit out of her when she was a child, telling her he despised weakness in any form, and no child of his was going to show him up in public or private. She grasped her fingers tightly, and waited.

'You've never been a particularly satisfactory child, but your behaviour right now is a disgrace! What were you thinking of when you took up with Barton? Don't you understand he was responsible for your brother's death?'

Kate, hurt and more than a bit shattered under his look of acute dislike, felt she had to try to justify her actions.

'But is he? No one else seemed to think so at the time. He showed me the tape of the race. . .'

'I say so!' He leant forward until his face was only a few inches from hers. 'Ace Barton not only killed my son, he helped to ruin him. Who introduced him to gambling in the first place? Ace Barton, that's who!'

'But Daddy, that's not fair. Eddie always liked betting on things, even when we were children! Why, I remember he always used to make me wager my pocket money —— ' She was interrupted.

'That's something quite different!' He made a sweeping movement with his hand, as if what she'd said was of no interest.

'I don't see ——' Kate started again.

'No, you don't, do you? You never have. . .'

Kate half recoiled from his expression. 'What do you mean?' Her voice wavered slightly.

'Oh, forget it!' Her father lay back in the big squashy leather chair and closed his eyes for a moment, before opening them again and fixing them firmly on his daughter. 'Listen, Katharine. You have a chance maybe to undo some of the damage that man has caused our family. I want to be sure you'll take it, so I'm going to handle the situation from now on.'

Kate felt a little faint. 'Handle what situation, Daddy?'

'Why, your marriage, of course! Do you think your mother and I are happy hearing you described as Ace Barton's latest tart?'

Kate blushed scarlet. 'I'm not! That is ——'

Her father interrupted sarcastically. 'You're not his girlfriend? Don't bother to lie, girl, it's written all over you!'

'Daddy, you don't understand. Ace has no intention of marrying me!'

Once more her father gave her a scathing look. 'I know that!'

'Well, then, why are you doing all this? Because he's not the sort of man you can bully. . .'

'I think I can handle it!'

Kate, looking dubious, watched the satisfaction in her father's face, then she remembered just exactly how Ace had managed to get her to do what he wanted. How could she have forgotten? She went pale.

'Daddy, there's something else. . . I'm sorry, but Ace has got some of Eddie's IOUs. That's really how he persuaded me in the first place to pretend. . .' Her eyes filled with sudden tears.

'Don't cry; you know I can't stand it!' Her father then leaned forward to give her a little shake. 'Are you trying to tell me that Ace blackmailed you into becoming his lover?'

Kate winced. 'No! Yes. . . Oh, I don't know. . .'

'Make up your mind, Katharine. This is potentially serious. Did you see the IOUs?'

'Yes, yes, I did. He showed them to me in his flat.'

'How much for?'

'Thirty thousand pounds!'

Her father sank back into his chair, a look of satisfaction on his face. 'Didn't you realise that after five years it isn't possible to claim on someone's estate?'

'He said he could pursue the matter, and he intended to do so, unless I —— '

'Good God!' Her father sat up straight. 'I never had much time for him when he was young, but I never guessed he'd do anything as rotten as this!'

'No, Daddy, you don't understand! He didn't use them to force himself on me. That wasn't what he wanted. He said he needed me to pretend to be his girlfriend to protect him from the bimbos.'

'Are you trying to tell me he's not your lover?'

'No! Well, yes, he is now, but that was my choice. . . He didn't touch me.'

Her father's face screwed up in a mask of hatred.

'My God, he's a clever bastard, but this time he won't get away with it, I'll see to that!'

Kate looked at her father with horror. 'What are you going to do?'

He turned to look at her, almost as if he'd forgotten she was there. 'Do? Why, I'm going to do what I set out to do at the start—I'm going to make sure that bastard marries you!'

Kate began to have the feeling that she was caught by forces stronger than her, that she was in the power of some strange vortex that was spinning her around so fast that she no longer knew how to keep control. First she had allowed herself to be manipulated by Ace, and now her father was trying to do exactly the same thing.

For the first time in her life she forced herself to stand back, to try to look at her father impartially. All her life she had striven to please him, loving him with no proof of any affection given in return. She realised that he had to be the root of her insecurities, of her inability to believe that anyone could ever love her in return. Quite without thinking, she asked the question that burned in her mind.

'Why do you hate me so much?'

'Because you're not my daughter.' His reply was so matter-of-fact, so lacking in emotion that she found it hard to believe.

'How do you know?' she whispered.

'Because when your brother caught mumps before you were born he gave it to me. It made me sterile.'

'Oh, God!' Kate put one hand up in front of her

mouth. 'Do you know? I mean, has Mummy. . .?' she floundered.

'You mean has your mother told me who he was? No, she hasn't, and, before you ask, no, I haven't bothered to find out!'

Kate looked her disbelief.

'All right!' Her father gave an angry gesture. 'I gave you my name in exchange for your mother remaining as my wife! I didn't want her walking out on me, leaving me looking a fool! She agreed, so there's nothing more to be said.'

'You really don't know who my father was?'

The man sitting opposite her looked shifty, but she could see from the set of his jaw that he'd no intention of telling her his suspicions.

'I'm legally your father. You haven't any other. You've been mine all these years. I've paid for your education, fed and clothed you. You owe everything to me, do you understand?'

Kate shut her eyes. She wanted to weep at the pity of it all, then she opened them again to stare at him. 'I owe you nothing! You made my life a misery.'

'You always were an ungrateful little bitch. Still, if your father was the man I think he was, then I suppose I shouldn't be too surprised at the way you've turned out.'

'And who was that?' Kate's eyes were hard and dry as she watched the bitter man sitting opposite her.

'I'll tell no tales. You'd better ask your mother!' he sneered.

'I will, when I get home,' Kate replied, 'and the sooner I do it, the better.'

'You're going nowhere until we've sorted out this mess with Barton!' Her father caught hold of her wrist in a savage grip.

'Take your hands off me!' Kate fired back. For years she'd been so meek, so biddable to this man, and all for what? He had hated her, and subconsciously she must always have known. That was why she'd striven so hard to be a success all her life. She'd tried to change his feelings for her. Wasn't it about time she put him through some of the agony he'd caused her? Gave him a small taste of what she'd had to suffer?

'You're not going to use me any more,' she told him quietly. 'I'm not interested in being cannon fodder in this feud you're having with Ace.'

'You'll do what you're told, my girl!'

Kate shook her head. 'I don't have to do anything you tell me. Legally you can't force me.' Her eyes looked dark and there was a bleak expression on her face that was mirrored in the face of the man sitting opposite her. 'You're pathetic and obsessed and you won't face up to the truth that Eddie was never good enough to make the jump into Formula One! He at least knew it, but you wouldn't accept it. You forced him to race against his better judgement and wishes. You were the one who killed him, not Ace Barton!'

There was a horrified silence between them, until her father leaned forward and slapped her hard across the face.

'Bitch! What do you know about it? You've been listening to loverboy, that's all!'

Kate rubbed her cheek thoughtfully, but now her dark eyes had lit with an inner fire.

'Everyone knew in the business at the time,' she continued remorselessly, 'but you had such a problem with your ego you couldn't or wouldn't accept it! I think Eddie was frightened, and that's why he gambled so heavily at the end.'

She watched the play of emotions on her father's face and knew her words had struck home. 'So I'm not going to stand by and let you use me and destroy me as you did my brother!'

'Brave words, Katharine, but how do you think you're going to stop me?' William Ash had lowered his head, and reminded Kate rather too forcefully of a bull about to charge.

'You can't exactly go ahead if I refuse to marry Ace, can you?' she answered defiantly.

'No, but if you refuse I'll reveal to the Press just how he blackmailed you into being his mistress. That'll go down really well with his sponsors and Carlisle Flint. In fact it might just finish him for good!'

'Why do you want him to marry me?' Kate was cornered and it was clear he knew it.

'I'm starting up again. Opening a new garage. I need his name to help me get going. If he's married to my daughter that'll kick-start me right back in the business, but if you won't play your part in all of this then I'm just as happy to bring him down. . .'

'I'll deny every word!' Kate spat back at him. Her

father once more lay back in his chair, and there was
a singularly triumphant smile on his face as he
brought out of his pocket a small tape recorder.

'It's all there, girl, every word! You can try to
deny it if you like, but it won't get you very far when
I play this tape back to the Press!'

Slowly he stood up, towering over the hunted-
looking girl. 'If you do what I tell you, Katharine,
then there's nothing to worry about, is there? Don't
forget it's in my best interests that the two of you get
together and make it legal! You'd better warn him
that I'll expect to see him some time tomorrow, if he
doesn't feel up to an interview this evening, that is!'

He walked away to the desk, collecting his key,
and as he walked towards the lifts he flicked a quick
glance back to the girl who'd been brought up as his
daughter. There wasn't the faintest trace of pity in
his face as he saw the defeated posture, just a
glimmer of satisfaction that his own plans were
starting to go well for a change.

Kate sat quite still, trying hard not to let the panic
that she felt overwhelm her so that she ran screaming
out into the still hot afternoon. The long hot Spanish
summer had baked the earth into a hard and unyielding soil that reminded her of her father. She tried to
feel pleased that she hadn't descended from such
uncompromising stock, but it was still a shock to
have been told that William Ash was not her father,
and that Eddie had only been her half-brother.

She longed to get home, to question her mother,
but her brain would not let her hang on to these
indulgences. She had to face up to the fact that her

father meant business, and that once more Ace was going to be put into an impossible position because of her.

Somehow she doubted that he'd now ever believe she was innocent of her father's plans, and that, if her father was successful in forcing Ace's hand, she would be the one who would suffer. She couldn't help but wonder why fate had insisted that these two powerful men should have insisted on using her to gain their own ends — her father for a return to power and motor racing, Ace for sex, because she now realised he'd wanted her all along. He'd just been rather cleverer and more subtle at how he'd gone about seducing her, even ensuring that she'd initiate the first moves.

She could see no way out of her problems. If she warned Ace what her father expected of him he'd laugh in her face. If her father played the tape of her conversation, as inevitably he would, then, whatever the outcome, their relationship would have been dealt an overwhelming blow, one, she was sure, that could never be overcome. With a sense of impending doom heavy on her shoulders, she went up to their shared suite to have a long, relaxing shower before preparing herself for the fireworks that would inevitably, as night overtook day, follow.

CHAPTER SEVEN

KATE had retreated to the safety of her room. She had no intention of being anywhere in sight when Ace returned. She'd packed her bags knowing that whatever else happened she had to go back home to find out from her mother just who her father was.

The discreet buzz of the phone caught her out. She'd intended not answering, but habit overruled her good intentions.

'Kate? I want you down at the track as soon as possible. Pack up my gear as well as your own. We're getting out, fast. I've got a helicopter due to pick us up in half an hour, and the *Citation*'s on stand-by. got it?'

'OK,' she agreed reluctantly, but inside she was conscious of a reprieve. Did this mean she'd get away before her father caught up with them? She ordered a car from the desk. The bill had already been taken care of, she found out as she asked a porter to help with their bags. At least Ace travelled light so there wasn't too much luggage between the two of them.

Too frightened to brave the front of the hotel, she found the staff stairs to escape by, and she hid behind a peculiarly luscious tropical plant until she saw the porter waiting perplexedly beside the taxi she'd ordered. Quickly she gave him a tip, also a message to be delivered to William Ash, warning him that

148

she'd be in contact with him as soon as she knew
where Ace planned to base himself.

In the taxi she discovered that Ace had won the
Spanish Grand Prix, but only just. Dino had broken
down, and it had been one of the best races of the
whole season, but then maybe the driver was preju-
diced, she told herself sourly. Oh, well! Maybe Ace
would stop blaming her personally for all his problems with the car.

The only good thing that had happened to her
today after her meeting with her father was that she
now no longer had her headache. It was strange to
be driving against the press of people leaving the
Jerez track, but she was hardly aware of her surroundings any more; soon she'd be seeing Ace again,
and, in spite of his bitter attack on her before the
race, at least she had known deep down that he
wasn't ready to part from her.

There were still huge crowds of people hanging
around the paddock, and Kate had quite a time,
burdened as she was with the luggage, to push her
way through. Luckily she appeared so insignificant
with all the bags that no one bothered to give her a
second glance. She used her pit-pass to gain entry,
then made her way towards the motor home Ace
used.

She noticed he'd showered and changed, as he
came out to meet her, grabbing his bags from her
limp grasp.

'OK, let's go. . .' He set off at a fast lope, leaving
her amazed that he still had enough energy to move
so quickly, but also puzzled. It was quite unlike Ace

to have left her to carry her own baggage, but of course he'd had a hard race. With a mental shrug she tried to ensure she kept up, knowing that nothing irritated him more than to be kept waiting even a second when he was in this mood.

The blades of the helicopter were turning at low revs as Ace bent low to put in his bags. He backoned to her, but Kate had stopped, turned to stone by the sight of her father talking earnestly with Mike Booker.

It was Ace's hand on her arm that swung her round to meet him, her face full of frightened guilt. He appeared not to notice, just taking her bags.

'Duck!' he called, pulling her after him. Her last view of Jerez, as the helicopter took off, was her father and Mike, both waving, their clothes whipped into a frenzy as they took off.

Kate sat in the back next to the luggage, but Ace had stationed himself in front with the pilot. It wasn't possible to have a conversation unless her earphones were connected, but this was the least of her worries at the moment.

So her father, it seemed, had wasted little time after leaving her. She sat in a fury of indecision and worry, wondering if he and Ace had met. Surely there'd been too little time, but then her father wouldn't have needed much time, would he? She shivered as the helicopter flew them towards the airport, once more totally oblivious of her surroundings.

It wasn't until the *Citation* had taken off that Kate was made frighteningly aware that her father had indeed been busy on her behalf. Ace sat opposite her, his face a mask; only the eyes glittered strangely, betraying his anger.

'Well done, Kate! You and your father have been very clever. I congratulate you.' Her eyes had flown to meet his, then dropped at his sarcastic comment as her cheeks became stained with an ugly red. 'Yes, you may well blush, sweetheart. You've been clever enough to catch me in a honeytrap partly of my own making! My God! You and your father, you're two of a kind, aren't you?' He ignored her anguished protest.

'I understand you're going straight home to Mummy and I shan't see you again until we meet in front of an altar. . . Your father insists everything is to be done properly, as befits his daughter, of course. . .' Ace's voice was slurred with exhaustion, but Kate's ear was finely tuned and she caught the bitterness hidden behind the carefully banked anger.

'I'm sorry, so sorry. . .' she murmured, her own voice almost suspended by tears.

'You're sorry! Quite frankly, my dear, at the moment I don't give a damn what your feelings are. You're on your own until I'm forced to take responsibility for you again. Make your own arragements for travelling home to Mummy. We are due to land at Gatwick, by the way. Now if you'll forgive me——' Kate could hardly bear his sarcasm '—I'm going to crash out. Its been quite a day one way and another, but after the performance at Estoril I suppose I should have expected it.' The brilliant blue eyes, hardly dimmed by his all too evident tiredness, shut, leaving Kate with tears pouring down her face as she gazed silently and unseeingly out of the window.

'Darling!' Her mother greeted her with a hug. 'This is wonderful news. Daddy rang to warn me. . .'

'Oh, Mum. . .' Kate hugged her mother in return, grateful for the warm body contact between them, but she couldn't stop herself from crying.

'Why the tears? Come on, you need a stiff drink. It's all that travelling and the excitement, I expect. Dump your bags, dear, we'll take them up later. Now, what's it to be? A glass of wine or something stronger?'

Kate blew her nose then smiled. 'A glass of wine would be fine.' She was aware that her mother had already had her first drink, and was on to her second, if not third glass of wine, if the bottle was anything to go by.

A fire was burning in the small grate to take the chill off the autumn evening. She looked around the small front room of the cottage that was now her parents' only home. If was a far cry from the big house that they'd lived in as far back as she could remember.

'Sit, darling, and tell me all about it!' Her mother handed her a glass of white wine, so generously filled that Kate was obliged to take a long sip before it was safe to put it down on the small table by the side of the chair. Her mother had filled up her own glass, but Kate became painfully aware that she was nervous as she sat opposite her daughter.

Kate knew she was probably going to be too blunt

for her mother, who liked everything to be wrapped in euphemisms, but she didn't feel able to go on playing her gentle games. This was too serious.

'Daddy told me he's not my father.' Her voice fell flatly into the warm pool of cosy light, shattering the illusion of family togetherness, of the prodigal daughter returning to the family hearth. Kate's heart twisted with pain as she saw her mother's familiar, guarded expression dissolve into fear.

'He promised. He promised me he'd never tell you. . .'

Kate came to kneel in front of her mother. 'Mummy, I'm sorry, but I asked him why he hated me so much. . .anyway, I don't mind — I'm happy he's not my father!' Kate tried hard to convince herself that this was the truth. It was difficult to deny the belief she'd held on to for so long.

'Oh, darling! You loved him so much when you were a little girl. And he, well, he was always a difficult man. . .'

Kate drew a deep breath. 'Tell me about my real father. That's what I want to know.'

'Yes, well. . . I met him on holiday. He was a young teacher. It was just a holiday romance really; he never knew about you, you know, never had any idea. Richard Redford was his name. He was always Richard, he hated being called Dick. We were fond of each other, but it was difficult because of Eddie, and your father. . . We hadn't been getting on too well, you see. But marriage, well, after all it's supposed to be for life, isn't it?' She looked at her daugher. 'He emigrated to Australia fairly soon after you were born. He'd no idea, you see, that the baby was his. . .'

'Oh, Mum!' Kate took one of her mother's hands and held it to her cheek, but her mother promptly sat up a little straighter.

'It's all right, my dear. It was so long ago, I've forgotten. . . Anyway, your father. William is your father in everything, except an accident of birth. You mustn't forget that!'

'I want to forget it!' Kate moved away from her mother. 'My so-called father is blackmailing Ace Barton into marrying me, and me into agreeing with his disgusting plans!'

The older woman put one had over her face. To the watching girl it became increasingly obvious that she could expect no more help. There was defeat in every line of her mother's body.

'It's no good, Kate. I can't fight your father. I never could. I'm sorry, but there it is. . .' She gave a helpless gesture with one hand.

Kate was overcome with compassion. Who knew better than her the strength of William Ash's bullying personality?

'It's all right, Mum. I'll fight my own battles. . .' Brave words, but she had the genes of the unknown Richard Redford in her veins even if he didn't show on her birth certificate. Ace might not love her, and he was furious at having his hand forced by William Ash, but there was something she could maybe start to build on, and that was telling him the truth about her birth.

She wouldn't stay down here in the country until

the wedding. No way! She'd go back to London and sort out her job with IMP for starters. If her father thought he was going to have her living at home, under his thumb, then he could think again. He might have bullied her mother into submission, but those tactics weren't going to work on her any more.

She spent most of the next day with her mother, but left before her father was due home, having checked that Ace was at his flat in London. She knew perfectly well that if she gave him any warning he'd find some excuse to refuse to see her, so, having dumped her own things in her flat, she went straight round to his, hoping to catch him before he went out.

She was lucky to get let into the building by another resident who obviously recognised her, so Ace was unprepared when she rang his doorbell.

'Hi!' She stood watching, quite unable to keep a hopeful expression off her face. The familiar blue eyes searched her familiarly, and she felt a wave of colour seep into her cheeks, but there was nothing particularly friendly in his welcome.

'What do you want?' Once more his face was a mask.

'I want to talk to you.' She gave him a tentative smile.

'What about?' His expression was as unresponsive as his speech.

'Please, Ace, won't you let me come in?' It seemed as if that was going to be in doubt as well for a moment, but then he swung the door wide in a parody of a silent welcome.

She walked past him into the big sitting-room and
he followed her, lounging insolently against the door-
frame as once more his eyes seemed to strip her. He
was wearing needle-thin black cords, the inevitable
trainers, and a black and white sweatshirt that bore
the logo of one of his sponsors.

'Well?' he queried insolently.

'There's something you need to know. William
Ash is not my father!'

His brows rose. 'So what's new?'

Kate couldn't believe it. 'You knew? How could
you know?'

'Eddie told me years ago. He found out when he
overheard your parents quarrelling one night.'

'Oh, God! He might have told me!' she responded
bitterly.

Ace shrugged his shoulders. 'He probably thought
it better that you didn't know. When did the old
bastard first tell you the truth?'

'In Jerez, while you were racing. . .' she answered,
her voice now totally devoid of emotion.

'You never knew until then?' Ace looked slightly
disbelieving. 'Oh, go on! He must have told you once
you were grown up.' Kate shook her head, and once
more there was a silence between them until Kate
broke it.

'He blackmailed me too, you know. He told me
that if I didn't agree to marry you he'd release that
tape of his to the Press. . .'

'How convenient!'

Kate couldn't ignore the sneer, but she faced it
with dignity. 'I knew you weren't going to believe

me, but it seemed only fair that you should know why I agreed to marry you.'

'You're so clever, Kate! I admire you, I really do. Here you are trying to have your cake and eat it at the same time. . . Maybe with nine men out of ten you'd succeed, but not with me, sweetheart, never with me! William Ash has trained you well. You might be his daughter only in name, but you've certainly learnt all his nasty, manipulative little tricks. I'll award you ten out of ten for trying. How's that as a consolation prize?'

Kate turned away so that he wouldn't see the pain in her face. His words hurt, really hurt, but she couldn't blame him.

'What do you want me to do, Ace?'

'I want you to be a good little girl and go home to Mummy and Daddy while I finish the season. After all, why shouldn't I enjoy my last months as a bachelor? I certainly don't want you hanging around my neck, if that's what's worrying you. Enticing you might be, but don't you know that variety is the spice of life?' He laughed unkindly at her shattered expression.

'Becoming Mrs Ace Barton might turn out not to be quite as exciting as you think. You might be going to become my wife in name, but not even your putative father can force me to live with you. I've bought a house in the country. Don't worry, it will live up to your expectations!' he sneered.

'I shan't expect my wife to travel the world with me, so that's where you'll stay. I shall visit just often enough to keep the gossips at bay. You needn't think you can keep your job with IMP either. I've already informed them confidentially that as my future wife you won't be interested in continuing to work for them.'

He straightened up, then casually walked over to her. 'Don't expect me to be a faithful husband, will you? You'll have to learn to be grateful just to bear my name. . . Now I think you'd better go. I've got a heavy date tonight, and it's not one I intend to break.'

His cruelty made it difficult to hide her hurt, and her big brown eyes swum with unshed tears. Ace kept his own eyes sapphire-hard, his expression negative in the extreme, and Kate knew she was totally defeated.

She stood like a dummy as her mother gave the last twitches to her wedding dress, trying to ignore the excitement that buzzed through the small house. Everyone seemed to be caught up in the general euphoria except the bride. She stood stiff and aloof, waiting passively for whatever was to come next.

Her mother, although distressed, was still far too much under her husband's thumb to give her daughter any but the most covert of support.

'It'll be all right, darling, you'll see. I know you love him. . .' One last kiss, then Kate was left alone in the small bedroom that she used when she came home. She stood in front of the mirror and looked back gravely at her shrouded image in the mirror. Her face seemed thinner, the high cheekbones more prominent somehow. Even through her veil she appeared beautiful but enigmatic.

'Katharine. . .it's time to go!' The call up the stairs made her compress her lips as she called on all her reserves of courage to face the ordeal ahead of her. Without answering, she left the room and came slowly down the stairs. William Ash stood and looked at her critically.

'By God, I never thought to say this, but I'm proud of you, lass!'

Kate said nothing, just allowed him to lead her out into the winter sunshine towards the waiting car.

It seemed as if her silence at last unnerved her father because he turned to speak to her just before they were to walk together down the long aisle. 'I know you love him, Katharine. You always have, haven't you? Right from the time when you were only a kid!' She allowed her eyes to smile into his — perhaps he was a little fond of her after all? He coughed a little nervously, before giving her a last look. 'Right, here we go, then. . .'

Kate stared rigidly ahead, refusing to acknowledge anyone. She refused even to look at Ace, although her body clamoured with a painful intensity as soon as he came to stand next to her.

All through the service she refused to look at him, keeping her eyes rigidly ahead on the stained-glass window that depicted Christ resisting Satan's temptations. She gave her answers in a low voice, almost feeling William Ash's relief as the vicar pronounced them man and wife.

She signed the register, still having avoided meet-

ing Ace's eyes, just shutting them when he kissed
her chastely on the cheek.

'Stop play-acting, Kate! This is what you wanted,
isn't it?' he whispered in her ear.

'No, it is not!' Her anguished reply appeared to
give him pause, but he had no time to follow it up,
as the organ began to play the triumphal entry of the
Queen of Sheba.

With a practised hand, she threw back her veil,
joining him as once more they faced the congre-
gation, which was waiting and watching for every
move, every twitch of facial expression.

There was no radiance to 'ooh' and 'aah' over, just
an appearance of aloof calm on her beautiful face.
Outside the Press cameras assaulted her senses with
the battery of flashes, but she didn't allow herself to
be flustered. Her expression remained enigmatic,
and it was quickly noticed that not once did she
publicly smile or acknowledge the man who was now
her husband.

Once in the car on their way to the reception, Ace,
still smiling at the hundreds of fans who had turned
up, spoke out of the side of his mouth. 'Loosen up,
will you? For your own sake try and look the part!'

'I can't see much point in pretending.' Kate had
her face carefully turned the other way. 'After all,
from what you told me before you went to Japan you
intend to go on living a bachelor life, almost as if I
don't exist.' Her voice sounded uninterested in the
whole thing.

Ace pulled her savagely into his arms, and possessed her mouth fiercely with his own. Kate's per-

verse decision not to co-operate held good. She felt is if she was in limbo, that somehow she was a disembodied spirit, one able to leave her body at will. But a small part of her cried that Ace seemed to have lost all sense of kindness and decency as far as she was concerned.

'You bitch!' he whispered as the car drew up in front of the country house hotel that her father had decided was good enough for the reception to celebrate the wedding of his only daughter to the reigning world champion.

He let her go and make repairs to her make-up, to try to disguise her bruised and swollen lips before the official photographs were taken. There they were photographed together, then just the bride, then joined by the best man, her parents and the ushers, but in none of them would she look at Ace, ignoring all commands to do so.

Afterwards she thought that perhaps only her father had really enjoyed her wedding, and, as he had engineered it and paid for it, then perhaps that was his reward.

Ace had warned her they would be leaving by helicopter, but where they would be going she had no idea. There was just one thing she had to get hold of before she left — the only wedding present she had been prepared to accept from William Ash. He came up to her room when she'd finished changing. She'd sent everyone away except her mother, and when he walked in she was ready for him.

'Give it to me!' she commanded. Mellowed by the

reception, he smiled at her, before putting his hand in his pocket to bring out the slim cassette.

'It's all gone real well, girl. I know you won't regret this day. There!' He handed it over, and she slipped it into her small black bag.

She gave him a fierce look. 'You've got what you wanted, but don't forget blackmail is a criminal offence.'

He looked totally taken aback.

'Don't speak to me like that, Katharine! I'm your father, for heaven's sake, and I'm fond of you, girl!' he spluttered.

'A man called Richard Redford is my real father.' She frowned. 'Are you really fond of me?' she couldn't help asking.

He spread his arms wide in a hopeless gesture. 'I've never been good at showing my feelings, but yes, I love you. You and your mother are all I've got left.'

A knock on the door interrupted him.

'Are you ready?' It was Ace.

'Goodbye, Mother. . .' Kate bent to give her one last kiss. Her expression made her mother's eyes fill with tears, but she said nothing. 'Yes, I'm ready.' She walked out of the door, grateful that her marriage had brought her perhaps one thing of value, and that was freedom at last from her belief that she'd never been loved.

She played her part to the end, grateful that Ace didn't seem keen on prolonging the agony. Her figure-hugging topaz velvet suit brought out the tawny lights in her brown eyes. Her hair, put up for the wedding, was hidden under a severe black felt hat, but its stark lines showed off her beatiful bone-structure. She looked elegant, yet slightly intimidating, her long legs in over-the-knee black suede boots as she followed Ace down to where the helicopter was waiting to fly them away from all their guests and the ubiquitous Press.

She was surprised to notice that they didn't make for either of London's airports; rather they seemed to be flying west into the rapidly darkening sky. She was even more surprised when they landed in a field near what looked from the air to be an L-shaped farmhouse with a great stone barn dominating one side of the farmyard.

Ace helped her out, leading her towards a Range Rover parked a discreet distance away. Once inside the car, she was greeted by a friendly-looking older man.

'Welcome to Bow Farm, Mrs Barton. . .sir. . .'

'Kate, I want you to meet Michael Reed. He and his wife are in charge of the farm proper. You needn't look worried. There's no stock up here any more. Michael and Sue run it all from the new buildings down the valley.'

Kate smiled and shook hands, but she felt wildly overdressed in her velvet suit and suede boots.

'This is the house I told you about, darling! I hope you're going to like it.'

'Well, it is rather difficult to tell at the moment because it's nearly dark, isn't it? But I'm sure it's beautiful.' Kate was peering out of the windows as they bumped their way on to a farm track and back to the house.

'Everything's been left exactly as you ordered, sir.'

'Thanks, Mike! I'm sure everything's fine. Come on, darling! I'd better live up to tradition and carry you over the threshold!'

'Don't be silly, Ace! That's quite unnecessary.' Kate neatly side-stepped him, and walked into the old farmhouse.

'You see, Mike, my wife's a modern girl. She doesn't believe in all these old traditions!' The older man laughed, albeit a little uncomfortably, Kate thought as she watched him drive away.

'Was that little display totally necessary?' Ace demanded, his voice edged sharply with anger.

Kate, avoiding his eyes, shrugged. 'I can't see much point in pretending, as I've already said. By the way——' She opened her bag and drew out the incriminating tape, which she put down on the round antique table which stood at the centre of the hall. 'You'd better burn this. I think it's genuine. You see, I refused to go through with the wedding unless he promised to hand this over before we left the reception.'

'So that's what the atmosphere was about when I came to collect you!'

'Oh, no! He was telling us that we were all he had left, that he did love me. Mind you, that could have been because he was happy he'd got his own way. He's incredibly self-centred, as my mother knows.' She still hadn't looked at her husband.

'That's a bit hard on your mother, isn't it?'

'I don't think so. She doesn't really mind any more. Now she takes comfort from the house and garden, so you see she doesn't really need me either.'

'Kate. Look at me!' She raised her eyes to his face, but he could see no flash of emotion there, nothing of the slightly vulnerable girl who'd tried to hide her hurt under an efficient exterior. He let his breath out in a harsh hiss.

'Do I gather you have plans for us?' he enquired, his voice sounding slightly sarcastic.

'There is no real "us",' Kate replied. 'Legally we are man and wife, but your lawyers can soon sort that out. I've no intention of bleeding you dry. I would be grateful if you would buy me a small house somewhere, perhaps near Bristol where I can find work.'

'I bought this house for you!'

'Oh, no!' She shook her head. 'No, you didn't buy it for me. You bought it as somewhere where you could keep me, and that's something quite different. You see——' she looked up once more and met his direct blue gaze '——you think I wanted to marry you, that I planned it all, but you were wrong, I didn't.' She looked at the disbelief on his face. 'I know you don't accept that, but spare me any more of your little plans for getting your own back, please! I heard quite enough of them at our last meeting.'

'Oh, so that rankled, did it?'

'Rankled?' She wrinkled her nose. 'I don't think that's quite the word to describe my feelings——'

Ace interrupted impatiently. 'For heaven's sake come in and sit down. I could do with a drink.' He pushed open a beautiful old oak door into what had to be the drawing-room. Long and low-ceilinged, with an enormous open fireplace, it exuded warmth and the sort of comfortable feel that a perfectly decorated interior could give when it was neither pretentious nor over-grand for the surroundings.

A bottle of Dom Perignon was waiting in an ice-bucket on the antique sofa-table. Kate looked around her with a sort of delight. She couldn't help it. Everything about the room charmed her, from the chintz curtains to the cherry-red linen sofas that flanked the enormous fireplace. The polished wood floor, the scattered rugs, the furniture, it looked as if it had been the same for years, yet Kate could see the newness of the sofas, the curtains.

'Here!' Ace handed her a bubbling glass. Kate had been so busy looking around the room that she'd rather forgotten why they had entered it in the first place.

'No, thanks! I'd prefer something soft.'

'Don't be stupid! One glass of this won't do you any harm.' Resentfully Kate took it from him before moving to sit down on one of the sofas.

Surprisingly Ace held his up to her in a mock toast.

'Don't!' she said fiercely, and he raised his brows in surprise.

'My beautiful wife!' There was an expression on his face that she couldn't quite fathom, so she brought the conversation smartly back to business.

'You've no need to stay here, Ace. I'll get out as soon as I can, of course. . .'

'Don't be so bossy! This is my house, not yours, yet. . . I'll stay as long as I like!'

Kate shrugged her shoulders. 'I was only trying to be helpful. You see, I don't expect, or want, anything from you, apart from a roof over my head.'

'What's happened to your flat in London?'

'William made me sell it. He loaned me half the cash to buy it, so he wanted the money back.'

'Tough!'

'Not really. Once I found out the truth I would have sold it anyway.'

'Are you trying to write me out of your life?'

She risked another quick look, then half shrugged. 'I suppose so, yes!'

'But *suppose*,' his voice lingered sarcastically on the last word, 'I don't want to be out of your life?'

'For a start I wouldn't believe you, and even if I did, to use your own word, tough!'

He lay back on the sofa and Kate was aware of a quality of menace, of tightly leashed rage. He looked an elegant stranger in his charcoal-grey suit, silk shirt and tie, and not least in the Gucci loafers he was wearing on his feet. She thought the whole thing had the quality of a dream, if the whole muddled mess was somehow totally unreal. She snapped her glass down on to a small side-table and stood up decisively.

'Is the bathroom upstairs?'

'Yes. . . I won't insult your intelligence by offering to give you a guided tour. There are three actually for you to choose from!'

Kate walked out, and climbed the shallow stairs that led so comfortably to the upper floor. This had been close-carpeted in a warm golden colour, but Kate guessed it covered more beautiful old wood floors. She was disconcerted to find that she walked into what was the main bedroom, dominated by a four-poster bed already turned down for the night. Another wood fire burnt quietly in the small grate behind a pretty mesh guard. A pretty pink and green chintz covered the windows and the curtains of the bed. It all looked delightfully cosy, with an en-suite bathroom, but Kate backed out of the room as quickly as if she'd walked into a pit full of rattlesnakes.

She found another bathroom, which was important, because the champagne was acting on her stomach just as she'd been afraid it would. She threw up until the nausea passed, just as it always did if she drank alcohol, but now it was almost as if her body already knew alcohol was bad for the tiny life growing inside her.

She looked at herself in the mirror. Mrs Ace Barton, with tumbled hair, and great black circles of tiredness under her eyes. It had been a strain, a terrible strain marrying Ace, but all would be well if she could escape before he found out her secret.

If she was honest, right at this moment she could think of nothing better than being able to collapse into bed, but it had to be alone. She might love her husband, but in exchange he'd never wanted anything from her except sex, and she wasn't even sure if he wanted that since he'd been forced into marrying her. Never must she put herself in a position where she might be tempted to betray the fact that she loved him.

She splashed water on her face, wishing she had her overnight case up here with her, wondering if it would be possible to make a deal with Ace. She'd better go down quickly before he started to get suspicious. She'd already decided to invent a tummy bug to explain any awkward disappearances she might be forced to make.

He wasn't in the sitting-room, so, interested in the house in spite of herself, she started to explore, his absence giving her the perfect right to do so. She found him in the kitchen, a big L-shaped room, like the house, dominated by an Aga cooker at one end, and a round table set in the shorter alcove. Warm tiles of what looked like baked, polished terracotta covered the floor in an intricate waving pattern that brought back memories of Portugal and Spain.

A delicious smell of casseroled chicken, heavy with herbs and garlic, hung in the air as Ace bent professionally over the oven.

'What are you doing?' Kate couldn't help herself. She'd never seen Ace showing the slightest sign of domesticity in either his London flat or the Monaco apartment.

'Just adding the finishing touches to our dinner. I thought you wouldn't mind eating in tonight?'

'No, of course not.' Kate shook her head. 'Do you need any help?'

'I thought you'd never ask. . .' He gave a grin, reminding her of the two short, intensely happy days they'd spent together. 'I think we'll eat in front of the fire, don't you? It'll be cosier than out here. We can put our feet up and watch telly.'

'OK.' Kate gave him a suspicious look, but he seemed to have recovered from the rage she'd been fairly sure he'd been trying to keep under control before she left the room. Perhaps he's happy because he's realised I'm not going to try to hang on to him, she thought sadly.

Once she'd discovered her pregnancy she'd had time to think, to plan. It had seemed to her at the time that this was all she was to be allowed of Ace, and so it became the most precious thing in her life. She guarded her secret carefully, terrified she was going to suffer from morning sickness, which might give the game away to her mother, but she'd been lucky. Alcohol and the smell of cauliflowers were the only two things that worried her.

IMP had paid her generously, and she'd hoarded the little money she'd made on her flat once it had been sold, but it still hadn't been enough to buy her somewhere to live. That was when she'd planned to ask Ace to buy a small house. Surely he'd be so grateful to be free of her that he'd agree?

She wished he'd stop treating her almost as if he was happy to have her around again. It would have made her task easier if he'd still been in the bitter, brutal mood that had possessed him after William Ash had delivered his ultimatum, but she didn't understand him at present. He ought to have been over the moon at her suggestion that she leave him, but instead it seemed to have made him angry. Was he perhaps not quite as indifferent to her as he had pretended after all?

CHAPTER EIGHT

KATE couldn't make up her mind all through dinner whether Ace was playing a deep game with her or had decided that as she was available, so to speak, he intended to continue making love to her. Deeply suspicious of his motives, she treated him with all the most obvious display of distrust of which she was capable, but her efforts seemed to leave him cold, so she decided there was only one course left open to her.

Ace was lounging on the sofa next to her, his shoeless feet now resting on the table next to the coffee, Kate's glances of distaste having been completely ignored. He was watching the end of the news on the telly.

'Hey, look, darling. That's us!' Kate had been half aware that the TV cameras were around, but she'd hardly expected their wedding to be tacked on to the end of the nine o'clock news. She'd married a sporting celebrity, so she'd expected a certain amount of attention, but she wasn't sure she appreciated Ace's rather smug pleasure at looking at himself. Her expression was jaundiced therefore as she gave it her attention.

'They must have been pushed to have put that in!' she told him scornfully, although she was secretly pleased to see that the camera had been kind to her. She also got quite a shock when she saw his face as

he turned to look at her on film. She sucked her
breath in angrily as she watched. 'You're such a
poseur! Such an actor. . . I suppose that look was to
appease your sponsors and your fans.'

He took hold of one of her hands. 'Is it so hard to
believe I could have meant it?' he asked her lightly,
but was there a suggestion of hurt behind the words?

'Quite impossible!' she snapped, snatching her
hand back. 'Particularly,' she continued, quite spoil-
ing the effect, 'when I remember all too well what
you told me last time we met, as well as. . .'

'As well as. . .?' Ace prompted, but Kate refused
to continue.

'So it's to be war, is it?' Ace turned off the news
by remote control, cutting off the picture of them
getting into the car on their way to the reception.

Contrarily this really annoyed Kate. 'You might
have had the decency to let it continue——' she
started to complain, but he interrupted her, smiling.

'I prefer to look at the original!' He gave her a
look calculated to have her on her knees in front of
him begging. Kate, forcing herself with the greatest
difficulty to resist his blatant charm, gave him back a
calculating half-smile.

'Trying to ensure that I remember you're now my
husband?' she enquired sweetly. She was surprised
to see his cheeks colour faintly under her taunt.

'And if I was? It's what I am, isn't it? I've been
forced to pay a high enough price for the goods, for
heaven's sake. Why shouldn't I enjoy them?'

'I don't think you've listened to one word I've
said, have you?' She continued angrily, 'I was forced

to agree to this marriage just as much as you were. I know your ego finds that hard to believe, but just because we had a good time together for a couple of days does not necessarily mean that I'm yours to play with whenever you feel like it!' She stood up, her indignation fuelling her feelings, all the pent-up resentment of years coming to the surface.

'I allowed William Ash to bully me most of my life because I loved him, because I thought he was my father! I knew I didn't measure up somehow, but I didn't know why, and I allowed that to spoil my life. Now I've found out that he isn't my father I'm learning to be free for the first time in my life, do you understand?' An expression of painful intensity twisted her features into passion.

'Then you came into my life and tried to do the same thing! You bullied me into becoming your girlfriend, so I had little choice but to obey, but now I've grown up. I've discovered I don't want to be bossed around by people like you! Expected to jump to it just because you click your fingers! You've made it very clear that you think I'm tarred with the same brush as William and that's fine by me! Go and find someone else to feed your ego, because I've had enough of dealing with men who need to bully women to feel good!'

Ace was on his feet by the end of this speech, his face white with anger. 'How dare you bracket me with your sordid relations?'

His raised voice was quite enough to set Kate off again. 'But that's just it! He isn't my father as you know damn well!'

'He might just as well have been!' Ace jeered in return. 'God, you're impossible! For all I know you've manipulated both William Ash and me into this whole situation!' His eyes suddenly narrowed as he looked at her, and there was a silence charged with meaning between the two of them. Kate wasn't slow to catch the implication.

'Oh, no!' She shook her head. 'You're not going to get away with that!' The depths that Ace seemed prepared to sink to just to hurt and wound her were the most painful things she'd experienced since the start of their relationship. So self-absorbed was she that she never considered for one minute that her words might have hurt him in exchange.

'Why not?' His voice was deceptively quiet. 'After all it was you who—er—spilled the beans, for want of a better phrase, wasn't it?'

'Give me a little credit for having no idea that my own supposed father was running a tape recording of our conversation!' she responded sarcastically.

'Oh, I don't know. . .You've known for years he was devious, and he'd never actually fallen over himself to be nice to you, had he? In your shoes I'd have expected him to come prepared with a big stick.'

'You mean I should have guessed he'd come prepared to blackmail us?' she enquired with mock sweetness.

'Well, it's not beyond the bounds of possibility, is it? You knew perfectly well that he held me responsible for Eddie's death as well as other things!'

Kate's eyes burned with a fury that was fast

reducing her to speechlessness. 'You're wicked as well as cruel and unkind!' she yelled, her feelings now quite out of control. 'I know you didn't want to marry me, but how do you think I was supposed to feel with the papers splashing pictures of you with Dara twined round you in Japan and Melbourne? Why did it have to be her?' Her voice rose high in anguish. 'I suppose I always knew you did it deliberately to hurt me, and it did! It killed whatever I felt for you stone dead!'

Ace's colour rose. 'I thought it might do you good to have a taste of your own medicine! You never once seemed to consider my feelings in all this, did you?'

'I never considered your feelings? Why do you think I bloody married you?' By now she was really yelling, letting her natural feelings show for perhaps the first time in her conscious life. 'All right, I was a fool to blurt out what I did to William, but I've paid the price, haven't I? Look, I can't stand any more of this. Leave me alone. . . I'll get out tomorrow. . .'

'There's no need. . .' Ace had pulled himself together, and conversely this made her own breakdown more apparent. Kate's shoulders were heaving under great sobs that racked her body. 'This house is yours. . .' he told her, but she was past taking in his words. 'For heaven's sake calm down, Kate, you're getting hysterical!' But his voice, even the meaning behind what he was saying, was beyond her. She spun round to face him. For a long moment their eyes remained locked in a fierce battle, until Ace's image began to shimmer in a sort of haze in front of her, then, quite without warning, Kate passed out; a great wave of blackness overwhelmed her, pushing all hurt and troubled feelings aside.

She came to almost immediately, Ace having caught her fall, then pushed her head between her knees. She felt nauseous, and, terrified she might be sick, she pushed away his hand so that she could hold her head up.

'Careful!' he warned. 'You might pass out again.' He tried to lower her head, but she resisted.

'Don't! It makes me feel sick.'

He continued to hold her, however, until the dry sobs that shook her body died down into something more manageable.

'I think it's time you were upstairs and in bed.' He looked at her expression, and his own face immediately became a blank. 'Don't worry. . .you can sleep alone — I can take a hint that I'm not wanted without you having to hit me over the head with it,' he finished bitterly. 'Tomorrow we'll try to sort a way out of this whole mess.' On this depressing thought they both went upstairs, and after another fight, which she lost, Kate was left alone in the big bedroom.

Some time during the evening Ace had brought her luggage up, but she was amazed to find, on opening cupboard doors, that all the clothes Ace had once bought her were neatly put away. As she'd returned everything he'd given her before he'd left for Japan this was quite a surprise.

She'd been so angry, after seeing the first picture of him with Dara, that she'd wanted to get rid of anything that had reminded her of their time together. She'd known that it was childish behaviour on her part, but she hadn't been able to help herself. Anyway, as they were summer clothes, and it had been the start of winter, that had helped make the decision an easy one.

She sat back on the bed, looking around her thoughtfully. Ace appeared to have gone to a great deal of trouble to make this place so pretty and welcoming. He'd certainly used an interior designer, and whoever it was had done a really remarkable job.

The next question was why had he gone to so much trouble and expense if he never intended to use this place as his base? It was nonsense to pretend it had been done solely for her benefit. This was a house that cried out to be lived in, was perhaps intended to be the home that Ace had never had as a child.

He'd obviously spent time here, perhaps as much as he could spare before their marriage. Was it still remotely possible that, in spite of everything, he'd been looking forward to having her here with him as his wife?

So OK, he'd probably never have married her if his hand hadn't been forced, or at least not so quickly, but didn't some of his behaviour indicate that perhaps he wasn't quite so averse to the situation as he pretended? Or was that wishful thinking? Oh, dear! Kate brushed her hand over her eyes. Really she was too tired to think rationally. What she needed was to sleep, and she tried to suppress the great mountain of self-pity that threatened to swamp her. This was her wedding night and she was going to be sleeping alone. It didn't help her at all to accept that this was by her own wish. Fleeting images of Ace masterfully entering her room, of him delightfully forcing his attentions on her slowly died as she finally made herself ready for bed. There'd been no need to unpack properly, because tomorrow she'd be leaving, of course.

She woke up, at first disorientated and unaware of exactly where she was, but memory soon came flooding back, and with it a drop to her spirits. Somehow she'd still hoped against hope that Ace might have come to her after all.

The morning looked grey and gloomy too, as if matching her mood, and Kate was reminded that January was hardly the most romantic month for a honeymoon in the English countryside. All in all she managed to add considerably to her feelings of inadequacy as far as Ace was concerned by the time she made her way downstairs towards the kitchen. How many brides were left to sleep alone on the first night of their honeymoon? If Ace had any real feelings for her he would have taken her prohibition as a challenge, and made love to her until she welcomed him joyfully into her bed.

She was surprised to find how late she'd slept in. Why, it was almost half-past ten, yet there was no Ace, nor any signs that he'd been downstairs before her. With a feeling of being ill-used she started to clear up the remains of last night's dinner, while drinking a freshly squeezed orange juice, then eating a bowl of cereal. Her husband, it seemed, didn't believe in having help around. Not, she told herself, that she was used to it, but having just married a man who had to be a millionaire several times over. . . She clamped down firmly on the thought, cross with herself. She wasn't a spoilt beauty with no brains, was she? No way! She was a working girl, and proud of it, and she intended to stay that way. . .

Still, as the morning advanced with no sign of him, Kate decided to do a little exploring of her own. She made a coffee as an excuse, then made her way back upstairs. She found him in a small single room that was obviously intended to be his dressing-room or study, furnished with a single bed, rows of built-in cupboards, and under the window a desk and chair.

He was dead to the world, so deeply asleep that she wondered what on earth he could have been doing half the night. She put the mug of coffee gently down beside him, all the time taking in the vulnerability of his sleeping face. He looked so very tired still, with shadowed unshaven cheeks, and there were deep lines running from nose to mouth that Kate didn't remember seeing before. Long lashes lay in a fan on his cheeks, and she longed to smooth the ruffled dark hair away from his brow.

She loved him so much that it was painful to just stand there watching him, and her eyes filled with easy tears. How could she walk away without even trying to give their marriage a chance? It would be like amputating part of herself, and she knew suddenly, and quite clearly, that she couldn't do it.

If it was her destiny to suffer in life, well, she'd had enough practice, hadn't she? Certainly not to the same degree of hurt, but a taste of what rejection was like at first hand. She'd survived years of William Ash's treatment of her, grown strong on her own. Surely, for the sake of her unborn child, she could survive again, accepting that to Ace she would only be just another reasonably attractive girl?

He still wanted her body, there was no way he could disguise that, and she, well, she would have to learn to be content with whatever crumbs he was prepared to let fall from his table. Once her baby was born, then she'd never be alone again. She would give to it all that had been withheld from her, pour out her infinite capacity to love knowing that for certain this time it would be needed and valued.

A tear fell and splashed uselessly on to the pillow, and she clumsily drew one arm over her eyes. Two arms caught her and drew her down into warmth and security as she continued to cry into the comfort of her husband's chest.

'Shush, baby, shush. . .' His strong arms rocked her, his hands stroked and soothed, till she felt comforted. It was like being a child again, but a secure one rather than someone like her who'd never been encouraged to cry out her troubles and fears. Some of the hard, heavy weight in her heart that had so wearied her seemed to lighten its burden as she gave up fighting him and, more importantly, herself. Her tears subsided into sniffs, but she still wasn't prepared to look up into his face. For a start she knew she must look a complete mess.

'You have the most glorious hair I've ever seen!' Ace's hands were playing with its silken looseness, but his voice sounded deep and husky with emotion. Kate said nothing, just cuddled a little closer to his bare chest, if that were possible, listening to the rapid beat of his heart. She shut her eyes as she felt his lips trace a light pattern of kisses that ended at the nape of her neck. A shimmer of remembered delight flooded through her body at his sensitive touch.

His hands reached under her jersey to find then undo her bra. A sound of satisfaction came deep from his throat as his hands fondled and teased her breasts until her nipples stood up hard and proud against the softness of his palms. 'You're so beautiful, my Kate. Do you know that?' He gave a great sigh of satisfaction as she tried to wriggle herself closer. Gently, under the comforting warmth of the duvet, he removed her jersey and bra, but his hands, not satisfied, sank lower, their movements purposeful as he removed her skirt to reveal the black woolly tights.

'Do you know I've always loved undoing parcels? Particularly when I know they're full of the most deliciously enticing goodies. . .' His voice teased, but there was an undertone of urgent desire which the light words couldn't quite conceal, and Kate smiled as she allowed her hands to explore his nakedness.

'Oh, Kate! I've missed you so much. . .' he groaned.

She was surprised. 'Why? You had Dara. . .'

'Don't!' His mouth found hers possessively, forcing hers apart to respond to his hot-blooded invasion. Kate gave in willingly, hearing the revulsion behind that single word with pleasure. She allowed him to slip off her tights and the soft lace briefs beneath. It was wonderful to be so close to him again, to feel no barriers between them, and he wasted little time before possessing her with such quick, hot urgency that she was left behind. But she was filled with such tenderness that she cradled his head as he lay against her breasts and whispered, 'I'm sorry, my darling, I'm sorry. . .'

To Kate it was more evidence of her importance to him, and her treacherous heart gave a leap of hope. He'd missed her! In spite of having Dara available. But it seemed Ace hadn't finished with her yet, and soon she was incapable of any thought at all, rational or otherwise, as he took her once more to the edge of paradise.

Afterwards they lay together and Kate was amazed at the expression of tenderness on his face as he looked at her.

'Do you know I really thought I'd blown it?' He spoke softly. 'I thought, well, let's just say that last night was something I never want to have to live through again. . .'

Kate blushed under his look. 'Well, if it comes to that I wasn't too happy either!'

'Are you trying to tell me that if I'd come to you you wouldn't have sent me away with a flea in my ear?' He couldn't disguise his amazement.

Kate wriggled a little uncomfortably.

'I suppose so. . . Yes!' she finished decisively.

'I ought to beat you! Do you have any idea of what you put me through yesterday? An unwilling bride. . . Oh, yes! You made your feelings crystal-clear. If I hadn't been so besotted and obsessed to the point of madness I'd have called the whole thing off!'

Kate stiffened. Had he said what she thought he'd said? He dropped a kiss on to her half-open lips and grinned. 'Now don't tell me you're surprised?' But it was obvious to even the meanest intelligence that surprise was the least descriptive word to be applied to her. She looked totally shattered.

'Didn't you guess, my beautiful idiot, that I've been crazy about you from the first time I saw you standing outside your hotel bedroom in France?'

'No, how could I?' She was in a daze. 'Anyway you said foul things to me then!'

He bent his head to kiss her. 'Yes, I did, didn't I?' His lips once more teased hers. 'So clever that you are, my darling, didn't you guess that was a typical bachelor's reaction to danger? I knew even then that if I went on seeing you my days of freedom were numbered. I was so frightened you'd walk out of my life again that I sank to ignominious depths to keep you close to me.'

Kate stared back at him, hardly daring to believe what she'd just heard. 'Are you trying to tell me that's why you threatened me with Eddie's IOUs?'

'Partly, yes. . .You had me in a fine old tangle of emotions. I wanted to believe you were as interested in me as I was in you, but. . .' He hesitated for a moment, and she took him up on it.

'You didn't quite trust me!' She saw the sudden

narrowing of his eyes and mouth. 'You needn't look so upset; it was mutual, you know!' Kate lay back against the pillows, her hair framing her face in a golden aureole.

'Oh, yes, I knew you didn't trust me and probably don't now. I've given you good reason to be suspicious of my motives.' The bitterness he was feeling twisted his mouth, and Kate tried to put things right.

'But if you're honest you'll admit that you weren't quite sure if I was going to make trouble for you!' There! Kate had put his worries into words. He bent to kiss her, his lips just touching hers in feather-light movements, as he traced the path of her jawline back to her ear.

'And you did!' he breathed. 'Not perhaps in quite the way I first envisaged.'

She looked back at him, her mouth slightly tilted in a half-smile, and put up a finger to lightly trace the outline of his mouth. 'I would never willingly have caused you problems,' she told him earnestly. 'So I was brainwashed by William about Eddie's death, but even so, whatever I believed, I would never have been able to hurt you!' Her eyes looked enormous in the aftermath of making love, great limpid pools full of warmth and love.

'And if I weren't the biggest idiot I would have known that, right from the start. Your honesty shines out of your face, my darling. It isn't your fault that cynical men like myself won't let themselves believe what they see! I just wish you could believe that Eddie's death was an accident and nothing to do with me.'

She could see how that hurt him, and put up a quick hand to stroke his cheek. 'But I do! I know now that it wasn't anything to do with you. I'm quite a logical person, you know. Once I'd seen the recording of the race I knew, although perhaps I didn't want to admit it straight away.' She smiled in apology. 'You see, then I didn't want to believe my father was wrong.'

Ace half sat up to look down at her, but his face was full of trouble. 'When you were shouting at me last night I realised, perhaps for the first time, just exactly what you'd gone through all your life. I'd no idea, you see, that you saw my treatment of you as a reflection of your father's, just another variation of the same problem.

'That's what kept me awake last night — facing up to the fact that my behaviour, anyway as far as you were concerned, was as devious and manipulative as anything that William Ash could come up with. I didn't really blame you for not wanting me to come near you, but it wasn't a particularly pleasant experience to realise that I'd put someone I'd loved through such an appalling time. I made a pact. I promised myself I wouldn't come near you again unless you wanted me to, that the ball would always be in your court, and that if you chose to kick me out of your life for good, then I'd respect that wish, even if it'd half kill me to do so. Kate, you've got an awful lot to forgive me for, haven't you?'

Kate knelt in front of him, placing both her hands round his face. 'I've run up a few debts myself, you know! I suppose I have to admit that I was stupid to speak so frankly in front of my fath. . .William. . .'

'Accept it, Kate! He was the only father you've ever known, so it isn't a crime to refer to him that way! Anyway, whatever I may have thought about his methods of bringing it about, I'll always be grateful to him for my wife!' He looked at her, the brilliant blue of his eyes narrowed and intent. 'You really do forgive me, Kate?'

'Don't be silly! Why, I've just as much right to ask if you'll forgive me.' She gave him a smile that showed she was still a little insecure, still not quite believing that Ace loved her.

'We're quits, then. . . Oh, my Kate! I do love you!'

Now was the moment she had been waiting for. She must pluck up courage and tell him. 'Ace. . .' She looked up at him and her eyes were troubled. 'There's something. . .'

His eyes hardened, as he looked into her troubled eyes. 'You can forget Dara! I let her tag along, but, if it makes you feel any better, I didn't sleep with her!' Kate looked bewildered, and he gave a great sigh.

'I know it's pretty unforgivable behaviour. I hoped if you saw her with me you'd be jealous! I thought you might even come round to the flat, and we'd have a row, and then everything would be OK between us, but all you did was send back your clothes.' He gave her a brooding look.

'I was so mad when your father tried to twist my arm. I thought at the beginning that you were working with him, that it was your revenge for Eddie's death.

I didn't even want to listen when you tried to explain. . . You see, it hurt me to think that you hated me, that you could have been conspiring behind my back with a man like William, but then I began to think a little straighter.

'If you'd really wanted to hurt me, you'd have let Ash go ahead with the publicity, would have backed him up, and I wouldn't have been able to deny it because it was all based on the truth, but a twisted truth! By the time I'd worked all that out, you'd gone, and in a way I didn't want to be beholden to you. It would have meant admitting to myself that I was wrong. . . Anyway, I told myself that once we were married it'd all be OK. You taught me quite a lesson yesterday!'

'Oh, Ace! Why were we such idiots?'

'You're very generous. . . What is it, Katie? What's bothering you?'

'I. . .we're. . .going to have a baby!' she finished in a rush, then, not daring to look into his face, studied his chest.

There was a silence, and, unable to bear the suspense any longer, she raised her eyes. What she saw mirrored there threw her into a panic.

'What is it? What's the matter?'

'Is that why you married me?'

Kate was given an insight into such a deep well of insecurity that she collapsed against him with relief. How was it possible that Ace, world champion, could feel so inadequate in his personal relationships?

'Darling Ace. I love you. I always have, ever since I was fifteen. There's never been anyone else for me. . .' Her voice sounded sure and certain to the man next to her.

'Really?'

Kate still found it hard to believe that this single-minded, dedicated, successful career man could be so uncertain of himself. Maybe it explained all those girls in his past as well. She gave him a little shake.

'Yes, really! And no, it won't make any difference to my love for you. You'll always come first in my heart, that I promise. . .'

They looked into each other's eyes, Kate's now full of warmth and such love that Ace picked up each of her hands, and solemnly kissed them.

'I guess I'm a lucky guy, and so's junior. . .You know this is going to take quite a bit of getting used to,' he complained. 'How much longer do we have alone together?'

'About six months. . .'

He smiled back at her. 'Do you want me to give up racing?'

She looked her surprise. 'No, why should I?'

He laughed outright then. 'Katie, you're a girl in a million. Goodness only knows why you picked on me!'

'Aren't you forgetting something?' she teased. 'I didn't!' He laughed, but she was pleased to see that he was fast becoming his normal self, this unwonted display of humility being hidden, perhaps only ever to be shown again to someone as close as her.

'We won't hold you back, me and the baby. If you'll let me, I'll come racing with you — if you'll make me part of the team?' she finished a little anxiously.

'You still want to be my chief fuel technician?' he teased, but she gave a mock pout.

'I can think of other and better things. . .'

'Sounds exciting. Why don't you demonstrate some of your ideas right now and I'll let you know how interesting I find them?'

'OK.' It was her turn to laugh softly, throatily. 'What about this, and perhaps this. . .?'

'That shows great promise, Mrs Barton. Now I also had in mind something along these lines. . .' Kate giggled. Ace gave her a mock frown.

'Now, now, Mrs Barton. I expect my employees to keep their minds on the job! This is a very important position you're after, I shall have to be very thorough in checking whether you're up to it. Of course the first thing we have to find out is whether your heart is in it?'

'Yes, boss! And I'm a quick learner, so they tell me,' Kate responded with an innocent look.

'Hmmm! Of course you have to love your work to do it well.'

'I don't think I'm going to have any problems in that department,' Kate teased.

'Good!' His mouth hovered just over hers. 'So we'll start at the beginning, shall we?' The blue eyes burning into hers were carrying a very disturbing message, and Kate wriggled in delight.

'Yes, please!' she said.

Accept 4 FREE Romances and 2 FREE gifts

FROM READER SERVICE

Here's an irresistible invitation from Mills & Boon. Please accept our offer of 4 FREE Romances, a CUDDLY TEDDY and a special MYSTERY GIFT! Then, if you choose, go on to enjoy 6 captivating Romances every month for just £1.80 each, postage and packing FREE. Plus our FREE Newsletter with author news, competitions and much more.

Send the coupon below to:
Mills & Boon Reader Service,
FREEPOST, PO Box 236,
Croydon, Surrey CR9 9EL.

NO STAMP REQUIRED

Yes! Please rush me 4 FREE Romances and 2 FREE gifts! Please also reserve me a Reader Service subscription. If I decide to subscribe I can look forward to receiving 6 brand new Romances for just £10.80 each month, post and packing FREE. If I decide not to subscribe I shall write to you within 10 days - I can keep the free books and gifts whatever I choose. I may cancel or suspend my subscription at any time. I am over 18 years of age.

Ms/Mrs/Miss/Mr _____ EP55R

Address _____

Postcode _____ Signature _____

Offer closes 31st March 1994. The right is reserved to refuse an application and change the terms of this offer. One application per household. Overseas readers please write for details. Southern Africa write to Book Services International Ltd., Box 41654, Craighall, Transvaal 2024.
You may be mailed with offers from other reputable companies as a result of this application. Please tick box if you would prefer not to receive such offers ☐

mps
MAILING PREFERENCE SERVICE

Next Month's Romances

Each month you can choose from a wide variety of romance with Mills & Boon. Below are the new titles to look out for next month, why not ask either Mills & Boon Reader Service or your Newsagent to reserve you a copy of the titles you want to buy – just tick the titles you would like and either post to Reader Service or take it to any Newsagent and ask them to order your books.

Please save me the following titles:		Please tick	✓
THE SEDUCTION OF KEIRA	Emma Darcy		
THREAT FROM THE PAST	Diana Hamilton		
DREAMING	Charlotte Lamb		
MIRRORS OF THE SEA	Sally Wentworth		
LAWFUL POSSESSION	Catherine George		
DESIGNED TO ANNOY	Elizabeth Oldfield		
A WOMAN ACCUSED	Sandra Marton		
A LOVE LIKE THAT	Natalie Fox		
LOVE'S DARK SHADOW	Grace Green		
THE WILLING CAPTIVE	Lee Stafford		
MAN OF THE MOUNTAINS	Kay Gregory		
LOVERS' MOON	Valerie Parv		
CRUEL ANGEL	Sharon Kendrick		
LITTLE WHITE LIES	Marjorie Lewty		
PROMISE ME LOVE	Jennifer Taylor		
LOVE'S FANTASY	Barbara McMahon		

If you would like to order these books in addition to your regular subscription from Mills & Boon Reader Service please send £1.80 per title to: Mills & Boon Reader Service, Freepost, P.O. Box 236, Croydon, Surrey, CR9 9EL, quote your Subscriber No:................................... (If applicable) and complete the name and address details below. Alternatively, these books are available from many local Newsagents including W.H.Smith, J.Menzies, Martins and other paperback stockists from 9th July 1993.

Name:...

Address:...

....Post Code:..........................

To Retailer: If you would like to stock M&B books please contact your regular book/magazine wholesaler for details.